Star Struck

Second Edition

Star Struck

Second Edition

Mike Faricy

Library of Congress Control Number: 2023915129
paperback ISBN: 978-1-962080-25-5
e-Book ISBN: 978-1-962080-26-2

MJF Publishing books may be purchased for education, Business, or promotional use. For information on bulk purchases, please contact the author directly at mikefaricyauthor@gmail.com

Published by

MJF Publishing
https://www.mikefaricybooks.com

To Teresa
"Are you even listening, Mister?!"

Acknowledgments

I would like to thank the following people for their help and support:

Special thanks to my editors, Kitty, Donna and Rhonda for their hard work, cheerful patience and positive feedback.

I would like to thank Ann and Julie for their creative talent and not slitting their wrists or jumping off the high bridge when dealing with my Neanderthal computer capabilities.

Special thanks to Ann for her patience.

Last, I would like to thank family and friends for their encouragement and unqualified support. Special thanks to Maggie, Jed, Schatz, Pat, Av, Emily and Pat for not rolling their eyes, at least when I was there, and most of all, to my wife Teresa whose belief, support and inspiration has from day one, never waned.

Prologue

Delton Baggott looked around to make sure no one was eavesdropping on their conversation before he pushed the newspaper across the table and whispered to his brother. "I'm telling you, bro. They'll never catch on. You see this article, and he's right here in town, helped open that restaurant. Who in the hell is going to know, Clarence? We bide our time for the next few days. Find out where he'll be and make the grab. We just send a ransom note, and sit back 'til we collect the money."

Clarence nodded in agreement. He had to hand it to his little brother. Always coming up with a plan and, more often than not, they seemed to work . . . once in a while.

"I like it, man. We can make all the arrangements in here, put together a decent plan and no one will be the wiser."

"First things first," Delton said. "We need to come up with an out of the way place to hold him. I'm thinking that sleazy old motel out on Highway 5. The only folks that go to that place are probably renting by the hour."

Clarence shook his head. "Ain't gonna work."

"Why the hell not?"

"For exactly that reason. Everyone rents by the hour, suddenly we're there two, maybe three days, and wearing masks, telling the cleaning lady not to come in. Bad idea. We're liable to stick out like a sore thumb."

"You got a better idea?"

"Matter of fact, I do," said Clarence. "The lake place."

"The lake place? You kidding? No one's been there in at least two years. Hell, it's barely got electricity."

"Exactly. We head up there, make it livable, get rid of the mouse shit, turn the water back on, keep a low profile, no way anyone can track us. It'll be perfect."

The more Delton thought about it, the more sense it seemed to make. He was about to say something when one of the guards walked up behind them and said, "Okay, fellas, break time's over. Back to work, we need the entire mess hall mopped and then the hallway leading down to the cellblock."

They both stood, wiped their hands across the front of their orange jumpsuits, picked up the food trays, and carried them up to the counter. They slammed the trays against the inside of the garbage bin to dump the remnants before placing the trays on the conveyor. They made their way to the waiting mops and buckets in the far corner of the County Workhouse cafeteria. The room was large enough to feed two-hundred-and-fifty inmates at any particular time. At this moment, there were just three guards drinking coffee in a distant corner.

"Think about it," Delton said. "A few more days and we can take it easy for the rest of our lives." They smiled at one another, picked up the mops, and went to work.

One

I rang Heidi's doorbell Wednesday night, just after seven. She'd invited me over for dinner. She didn't mention it, but I happened to know the real reason she asked me over was she'd just broken up with her latest guy. I think they dated for six or eight weeks. I knew he was some high priced lawyer, but that was about all the information I had. Knowing Heidi, I was surprised she'd lasted that long. She liked things pretty black and white, and a high priced lawyer meant a lot of grey area, an awful lot.

I'd been through this before, close to a dozen times. The news of the break up would surface just after she got into her second glass of wine. On the first couple of breakups, there were lots of tears, but I hadn't seen any tearful reaction the last six or seven times. Now, it was just sort of a resigned sigh. She'd give me all the details over another three or four glasses of wine. Once again, I'd agree, whoever he was, he was really stupid, which actually was true. The night would conclude with an incredible hours long romp in her bed that would take me three days to recover from. I couldn't wait.

She answered the door wearing a tight white top about two sizes too small, no bra, and a skirt just a little wider than my belt. A diamond pendant dangled alluringly in her cleavage.

"Wow, what got into you? Right on time, for a change," she said, taking the bag with the three bottles of red wine. "Come on back, I thought we'd eat in the kitchen. I made ravioli."

We always ate in the kitchen, and she always made ravioli for these post-breakup dinners. I figured there must be something cathartic for her in the preparation process. By the way, the homemade ravioli was fantastic. The dining room would be off-limits for another two weeks as if she felt she somehow wasn't worthy. She set the wine bottles on the kitchen counter. I noticed she already had a glass going and made a mental note, number one.

"Oh, Dev, you are so sweet you always remember. A Sean Minor Pinot, my favorite. Oh my, 2014 vintage, aren't we special."

"Actually, there's three of them. I know you like it, and I feel like we haven't seen one another since forever. Guess you've been pretty busy. How are things going?"

"Well, with the economy going strong, I've been jammed at the office. Of course, the whole tariff situation is sort of hanging out there. There are predictions for everything from another recession to an even stronger economy. You know, I just keep my head down and continue working."

I knew for a fact, she'd forgotten more about the economy and business than I would ever know. She was smart, sexy, real sexy, and she could probably retire tomorrow if she wanted to.

"Here, I made some little hors d'oeuvres for us," she said, sliding a plate in front of me from across the kitchen counter. I had a pretty good guess what they'd be, goats cheese and prosciutto. It was part of her recovery process.

"Goats cheese and prosciutto," she said, taking one and tossing it in her mouth. "Do me a favor and open one of those pinots, okay?"

"You sure? We don't have to, and you can just hang onto them and save them for another night."

"The opener's in the drawer," she said, then drained her glass and slid it across the counter toward me. I opened the bottle, it was a twist off cap, then poured the wine through the aerator. It made a distinctive sound. Heidi took her glass, waited until I had poured mine, and then we clinked glasses.

"To happier times," she said and took a large swallow.

"Everything okay?"

"Yeah, not a bother. Come on, let's not rain on the parade."

I'd get the story halfway through the glass of wine.

It didn't take quite that long. Turned out, the guy was "a couple of years older" than Heidi. A partner in a high buck law firm downtown. He had a sports car, a lake place and, she found out, a wife and two kids. We were now finished with dinner, and Heidi was well into the second bottle of wine. Show time.

We were sitting on the living room couch. She was angled in the corner with her legs comfortably draped across my lap. The lights were turned down low, the drapes were pulled, and just in case things weren't morbid enough with Heidi asking a half-dozen times what was wrong with her, Leonard Cohen was playing on her sound system.

This is the way it always went, and after all the times I'd been through this, I was beginning to sort of like Leonard Cohen. Despite the morbid routine, he always seemed to eventually put Heidi in one of her sex-crazed moods, and tonight, I was going to be the beneficiary.

She drained her glass and reached for the bottle on the coffee table. She was slurring the occasional word and moving her head in a way that suggested it was a good thing she wasn't behind the wheel. She had passed the stage of using the aerator, and she filled her glass almost to the rim. She took a sip and dribbled red wine down her white top.

"Oh, shit," she said.

"Want me to get a paper towel or something."

"No, too late, damn it." She set her glass on the coffee table, sat up, pulled her top off and tossed it over her shoulder.

I didn't complain.

When her glass was about halfway empty she suddenly set it on the coffee table and said, "Okay, you ready?" Sounding like she was announcing the start of the second half to a football game. She swung her legs off my lap, waited for a few seconds to get her bearings, then shoved her hand around my belt buckle and led me into her bedroom.

The lights were off, but she already had a half dozen candles lit. A candle flickered on both bedside tables, and four more were evenly positioned across her dresser.

"Here, let me help," she said and proceeded to undress me. As I crawled onto her bed, she dropped her skirt on the floor, walked around the bed, and opened the top drawer on the bedside table.

"Ready?" she said, flashed an evil grin and then pulled out a large, battery operated appendage.

"Holy cow, Heidi, are you sure you can take that?"

She smiled, pulled out a black leather strap-on harness, and stepped into it. "Not to worry, sweetheart, it's not for me."

"Not for you? But, then . . ."

"Better take a deep breath," she said as she crawled on top of me.

TWO

The Green Door was a trendy, quasi-posh diner that served breakfast and lunch from six in the morning until half-past-two in the afternoon. It had a food and drinks menu, although, at just a little past ten in the morning, I was drinking coffee, black. Given the hour, the idea of a Bloody Mary or a beer sort of lost its appeal.

She saw me before I spotted her. Caroline Dillon, aka Caroline Travis, aka Caroline Moore, or, as I'd known her in high school, Sassy Aronson. If she was hot back in high school, she was scorching now, even after three marriages. She was dressed in tight-fitting Spandex leggings, black with a green maple leaf pattern, and nude-colored stiletto heels. Her small off-white top appeared to be strangling her surgically enhanced attributes. The top was low cut and barely covering. Her flat, tan stomach was enhanced by a multi-carat diamond that pierced her navel. She carried a double zip backpack that matched her Spandex leggings.

"Yoo-hoo-hoo, Dev," she called from across the restaurant and sort of jumped up and down. Immediately, every head in the place that wasn't already looking turned to stare. She headed toward me, strutting, one foot placed directly in front of the other, as if she were walking down a fashion show runway.

I read the lips on a fat guy two tables over. "Lucky bastard," he said and gave me the nod. I smiled back at him, then stood as Sassy approached. She leaned over and gave me a kiss on the cheek, followed up with a nibble on my ear lobe, stepped back, and scrunched her nose so I could admire her complete package.

"Mmm-mmm, you look great," she said, never one to tell the truth. She swung her backpack into the far side of the booth. I noticed it had a black leather patch stitched into the lower half of the pack with the name marc jacobs. I wondered if he was her most recent husband.

As she sat down, I smiled and winked at the fat guy.

He shook his head and shoveled in another forkful of syrup-soaked pancakes.

"Sassy, great to see you. How've you been?"

Not so much as blink. "Well, I suppose you heard. I'm divorced, again," she said, sliding into the booth across from me. She pulled a handful of paper napkins from the dispenser and a small spray bottle from the backpack. She misted some sort of disinfectant in front of her and began to clean the Formica tabletop.

"I might have heard something about the divorce. I don't really know any details," I said. I searched but couldn't find much more than an announcement on the internet.

"You'd think I'd learn, but these losers keep finding me. Fortunately, my attorney is very good. He's handled all my divorces, and when everything is all said and done, I've managed to come out okay."

'Managed to come out okay?' Clearly practice makes perfect. From what I knew, Sassy had never really held a job. She lived in an expensive top floor condo downtown when she wasn't spending the winter months in Florida or the Bahamas. She drove a dark blue Mercedes S 65 AMG coupe with a white convertible top. I couldn't afford the insurance, let alone the car, and on top of all that, she was head-turning, conversation-stopping, drop-dead, gorgeous.

"Hi, can I get you something, a coffee or tea. We've a nice chilled champagne?"

My waitress had suddenly been replaced by Teddy, the owner. A guy I sort of knew and who never, ever waited on tables.

"Mmm-mmm, I'd love a decaf tea . . ."

"Coming right up, I got just the one for you," Teddy said and grinned.

"Before you get that, can you tell me how it was decaffeinated?"

"How it's decaffeinated?"

"Yes, the tea, did they use ethyl acetate or methylene chloride? If they did, I wouldn't want to drink it."

"Oh, no, of course not. Well, I could check, I guess."

"Tell you what, maybe you better just make it a bottle of spring water, sparkling spring water. Pellegrino. I'll pour the bottle myself, please don't open the cap."

"Spring water," Teddy smiled and looked relieved.

"Pellegrino," she said.

"I'll be right back."

"Gee, sorry to hear about your latest divorce, Sassy," I said.

"Don't be. I took him to the cleaners. By the time I was finished, he was on his knees and willing to do just about anything to get a settlement. They always start out thinking they're going to win, and it always ends up the same. 'Course, Jerry Baker was presiding. He's been on the bench for all three of my divorces," she said and smiled.

"Jerry Baker? The same Jerry Baker you dated in high school?"

She smiled and shrugged.

I guessed the Honorable Judge Baker was in violation of a number of aspects of the law, and if Sassy's former husbands ever got wind of this, they'd have their attorneys filing appeals the very same day.

Teddy suddenly appeared with a glass of ice and a green Pellegrino bottle. "Your water, ma'am."

"Thank you," she said and flashed her brilliant smile.

"May I get you anything else?"

"No, thank you, I've my work out after this."

For a second, Teddy looked like he was going to of-fer to help with her workout. He smiled for a long mo-ment and said, "Please, call me if I can be of any service. Anything at all," he said and started to walk away.

"Teddy," I called and raised my empty coffee mug. He sort of frowned, nodded, and kept moving. I turned back to Sassy, now rubbing a napkin around the rim of her glass before filling it with sparkling water. As beau-tiful as she looked, I was getting the sense there might be some issues that trumped her physical appearance.

She frowned and said, "Mmm-mmm, one too many ice cubes in the glass." She took a spoon and removed an ice cube, placing it in my water glass. She carefully poured the Pellegrino into the glass and took a sip.

"So, you said you were having a problem but didn't elaborate."

She nodded. "Yeah." She leaned forward and whis-pered, "I didn't want to say anything over the phone. I think someone might be listening in."

"Really? Any thoughts who?"

"That list is long. You could start with my three ex-husbands. After them, there are a number of individuals I've dated who were naturally upset when I didn't want to see them anymore. I've filed restraining orders on two different people. I suspect I'm being followed. I've had a feeling someone has entered my home . . ."

"Your penthouse?"

"Yes, while I've been gone. Now, all that said, at the end of the day it is still just a feeling. Nothing that I can prove, yet."

"Have you called the police."

"Yes, and they were absolutely no help. I thought, under the circumstances, it wouldn't be too much to ask that they station someone outside my door, but apparently they were simply too busy to aid a taxpayer in need."

I tried to envision the poor cop who had to take the call. They're shorthanded, underpaid, and not getting a lot of respect even on a good day. I couldn't come up with a positive image. "Okay, so what did you have in mind?"

Three

We had just stepped off the elevator on the twenty-third floor of Sassy's building. It looked like there were just two units on the floor, one on either side of the elevator. Both had a keypad mounted on the door to unlock it. An antique credenza stood just opposite the elevator. It had a lamp on one end and a cut glass vase with flowers on the other, the flowers, mums, and daises, appeared to be fresh.

"As you can see, it wouldn't be that big of a deal if the police brought a chair and were comfortable while they guarded my door. I mean, I don't have a problem with them sitting down occasionally. It's not like I need them standing at attention all the time, but they weren't even interested."

I just nodded in response to her comment about it being no problem to station a cop at her door.

She input a five-digit code on the keypad, and the lock made a sort of grinding noise. She turned, gave me a sexy wink, and I followed her inside. The place looked contemporary, which usually isn't my thing, but I liked it. In the middle of the room was an open circular fireplace. A large copper dome hung over the fireplace, suspended by massive chains. The room had a white marble floor with a number of white throw rugs scattered around. The windows on the far wall were floor to ceiling, looked to be at least ten feet tall, and had a wonderful view of the Mississippi River valley.

A woman in a black skirt and top wearing a white lace apron suddenly appeared on the far side of the room. She was pushing a cart loaded with cleaning supplies.

"Oh, Carmen, I'm absolutely famished. Could you make me a piece of toast with marmalade, no butter? Thank you. Would you like something, Dev?"

"No, no, nothing for me."

Carmen rolled her cart back down the hall and disappeared through a doorway.

"Let me show you just one of the many things I'm dealing with," Sassy said, making it sound like there was a major hassle. I followed her around the fireplace, past the custom made white leather couches and down another hallway.

"Is there a bypass system to your front door lock?"

"A bypass system? You mean like a master code thingy or something?"

"Yeah."

"Not that I'm aware of."

"Who provides your security service?"

"A company named Elite Security, they were recommended. Are you familiar with them?"

"Only by name, I know they have a very good reputation."

She opened an oak door with an antique brass doorknob. The oak trim above the door featured a pair of carved, classic comedy-tragedy theatre masks. "This is my entertainment center," she said as we stepped into the room. There were three rows of four red, reclining theatre chairs, twelve in all. The floor sloped so that your view wouldn't be obscured by the person or the chair in front. A large painting hung on the wall opposite the chairs. She pushed a button on the wall, and the painting rose up into a slot in the ceiling, revealing possibly the largest flatscreen tv I'd ever seen.

"This looks really nice, Sassy. I'd probably end up in here all day long."

"I can't begin to tell you the difficulty I've had with this. I mean, is it too much to ask for proper sound and color?" She walked over to the tv and ran a finger along the edge, then looked at her fingertip, shook her head in a disgusted manner and sighed. "The dust, it just never ends."

I followed her out of the room and down the hall to what I took to be the master bedroom. The walls were a pale-pink, giving the room a cold kind of feeling. The bed was large, at least kingsize, and had two steps to get up to it, almost giving it the look of an altar. A pink bedspread, just a shade darker than the walls, covered the bed. The bottom of the bedspread was edged with white lace. I counted six pillows and eight stuffed animals lined up across the head of the bed. A framed oil painting of three naked people embracing hung on the wall above the pillows and stuffed animals. A mirror, the size of the bed, was attached to the ceiling and edged in a large gold frame. Along one wall were eight louvered doors, each with a six-foot mirror, presumably, storage for incidentals, since the entrance to the walk-in closet was next to the double dresser.

"Nice room," I said.

"No, it's a lovely room," she replied, correcting me. She suddenly glanced at her watch. "Oh, my toast." She hurried out of the room. I figured I was supposed to follow, so I did.

Carmen, the woman who had prepared the toast, was nowhere to be seen. Who could blame her? The toast, one slice, was perfectly centered on a white china plate. A white linen napkin, starched and folded, rested on the grey granite counter next to the toast. The crusts had been cut off the toast, and neither the knife nor the jar of marmalade were in view. I was beginning to wonder where Carmen was hiding and if there was room for two.

Sassy took a bite of toast and closed her eyes for a long moment savoring the taste. She finished the piece over the course of the next five minutes and never said a word. I just stood there leaning against a granite counter with my arms crossed, watching. She picked up the linen napkin, wiped her fingertips, dabbed at her lips, and said, "So, what do you think?"

"It looked like a nice piece of toast."

She stared at me for a long moment, not sure what, if anything, she should say.

"Sassy, your place seems reasonably secure. You have an alarm system, monitored by a reputable company. You're up here on the twenty-third floor, so it's not like someone is going to get in through a window."

"There's always window washers?" she said.

"Only once a year, I don't think they'd be an issue. You have a secure entry. I'd be willing to bet that the police have a file on your unit. In fact, the cop you talked to probably looked it up while he was on the phone with you and decided that if they placed security just outside your building, you'd be better served."

"But I haven't seen anyone out there. Certainly, no police."

"Exactly. They want to be undercover, so they can arrest any potential intruder rather than have them see a uniformed officer and simply move on to the next target," I lied.

Amazingly, she nodded, suggesting I actually made sense.

Four

I was back in the office looking out the window through binoculars at a couple of shapely young moms pushing strollers down the street. They were talking and laughing nonstop. They wore tight shorts and loose tops. Both babies looked to be very young, and, for the moment, asleep, at least until it was time to eat.

Not a bad life, just eat, sleep, and your pretty mom changes you. You're too young to worry about the economy, the government, or how your favorite team is doing, and the most beautiful woman in your life lifts her top and presses you close a number of times on any given day.

My cellphone rang. I glanced at the name, a bunch of letters that didn't make any sense, but answered anyway. Amazing what one does to get business.

"Dev Haskell."

"Hey, bro, long time no talk," the voice said and chuckled.

"You're telling me. What's happening, man?" I had no idea who was on the other end.

"You're not going to believe it, but I need your help."

"What's the problem? DUI? Wife having an affair? Someone's husband after you?" I was trying to place the voice. He sounded familiar, maybe. But I couldn't put a name to it.

"Nah, this is cool. Anyway, need your help, I can even pay you a couple of bucks. An easy gig, and it'll be fun."

"What kind of help?"

"Tell you what, I just pulled up in front of this place. Have to run in and get fitted. You know where Painful Pleasures is?"

"Painful Pleasures? That body piercing place?"

"Yeah, just off of Seventh Street. I've got an appointment. Meet me down here, and I'll fill you in."

"Yeah, okay, it'll be good to see you again. It's been a while, we can catch up, and you can tell me what you've been up to in the last—"

"Gotta run, man, see you in a bit," he said and whoever it was hung up.

"You got some work?" Louie Laufen asked. He was my officemate, an attorney, currently sitting in his office chair with his eyes closed and feet up on his picnic table desk. He'd been asleep, snoring, until a few seconds ago, as he spoke, his eyes remained closed.

"Work? Yeah, maybe. If I can figure out who that was. The voice sounded familiar, but I can't place it. I just wish people would say who the hell they are when they call."

"Well, don't forget to mention my name if he needs any sort of representation."

"Not to worry, once I figure out who it was."

I picked up the binoculars, did a quick scan up and down the street, but the women with the strollers had apparently disappeared around the corner. After a few minutes of scanning the empty apartment windows in the building across the street, I set the binoculars in my desk drawer and quickly ran through my rolodex, hoping to see a name that would spark a memory. It didn't happen. I hopped in my car, a 2013 Jeep Wrangler that had been on its last legs since it rolled out of the factory in 2013. It started on the third try, and I headed off to Painful Pleasures.

Five

It was hard for me to envision a business devoted solely to piercings, although that's exactly what Painful Pleasures was. But then what did I know? I conjured up a vision from my high school days. Maybe a tiny dark room with someone's older sister heating a sewing needle in a candle flame before she stuck it in your ear lobe.

I walked into a contemporary lobby with a carpeted floor and a fancy cherrywood receptionist counter and a black granite countertop. A half dozen people were seated in the lobby reading magazines while they waited to have holes put in them.

The woman behind the counter smiled at me as I approached. She had a number of shiny silver bars piercing both her eyebrows, and her ears looked like there were zippers along the outer edge. A red jewel pierced either side of her nose, a silver ring with a green stone pierced her bottom lip, and when she smiled and said, "Hi, how may I help you?" I noticed there was a gold ball implanted in the middle of her tongue. I wondered if the TSA folks gave her a hassle when she tried to board a plane.

"I hope you can help. I'm supposed to meet a client here."

She nodded, smiled, and said, "And the name?"

"Mmm-mmm, that's part of the problem. See, he called me earlier this morning and told me he had an appointment here and that I should meet him. I just, unfortunately, sort of blanked on his name."

"Bono?"

"Bono? The U2 guy?" I said.

She nodded excitedly.

"No, 'fraid not."

She clicked some keys on the computer and said, "Mmm-mmm, if I gave you a first-name would that maybe ring a bell?"

"It might."

"Jeffrey?"

"No."

"Constance?"

"No, it's a guy."

"Luther?"

"No," I shook my head. "Unless it's, Wink. A guy named Luther Winkler, but I haven't seen—"

"Yes, that's the name he's using," she nodded. "He's waiting in room three. Oh, lucky you," she said, grinned and pointed toward the hall.

Lucky me? "Thanks," I said and headed down the hall. I hadn't seen Wink since, well, I hadn't seen him for a lot of years. We used to run in the same crowd in high school before we went our own way. Last I heard he was doing some sort of construction work, framing or something. He was a short guy, blonde, blue eyes, always sort of looking for an easier way to do whatever we were doing.

There were a half-dozen numbered doors along the hall. In-between each door was a framed black and white photo of piercings and jewelry, perfectly centered on the wall. The photos had been professionally taken. None of them were revealing, just ears, nose, lips, and navels. Actually, the images were rather nice, with elegant jewelry, but if a needle was involved, that automatically left me out of the picture.

If there was a gunshot, I'm probably your guy. But anything involving a needle, forget it. I can't deal with it. I had a couple of dates with a woman who was diabetic a few years back. We seemed to be hitting it off until one morning at breakfast she casually gave herself an injection after which she had to spend the next ten minutes bringing me back around when I fainted and fell off the kitchen stool.

It dawned on me that Wink was always pulling practical jokes on guys. If that was the reason he called, just to have a laugh as I passed out and hit the floor watching his piercing, he had another thing coming.

I took a deep breath and knocked on door number three.

Six

As I opened the door, I kept knocking. A vaguely familiar sounding voice said, "Hey, you made it, bro. Long time no see, man," Wink jumped off the examination table as we shook hands.

At least, I thought it was Wink. He was wearing black trousers, a black t-shirt, and a black vest over the t-shirt. He seemed to have grown since the last time I saw him until I glanced down and noticed the soles of his shoes were about three inches thick. And, then, of course, there was the hair and those glasses.

The glasses were sort of rose or orange-tinted with wide frames. His once blonde hair was now dark brown, a dye job I figured, neatly trimmed on the sides and a little longer on the top. His beard was maybe a two or three-day growth. He looked like someone I knew or maybe knew of, but I couldn't place it.

"Wink, how you doing, buddy? It's great to see you. It must be almost ten years."

"Closer to fifteen, Dev, but who's counting? And from now on, you need to call me Bono."

"Bono?" I said as it suddenly all came together for me. "Holy cow. Yeah, the receptionist asked me if I was here to see Bono, but it didn't register." I stepped back and looked at him as he struck a pose. Yeah, he was a carbon copy. Absolutely amazing.

"You dyed your hair?"

"Yeah. And that's kind of why we're meeting here. I have to get my ears pierced like him."

"So, you're what? A double in a movie or something?"

"Oh, man. I wish. No, at least, not yet. I'm just trying to keep up the routine. You wouldn't believe the gigs I'm getting."

"Gigs?"

"Yeah, impersonating Bono. I've done a couple of bachelorette parties, a restaurant opening over on the west side the other day. In fact, it was written up in the paper. Did you see the article?"

"I guess I kind of missed that one."

"I gotta do a cover band gig Friday night at a bar in Woodbury. Ever hear of the band, 'U and Me'?"

I shook my head. "Sorry, but it's not really ringing a bell."

"Well, that makes two of us, but they're paying me a hundred bucks to show up and make the scene, you know like I'm they're big pal, Bono, and it's okay with me that they're playing all my music."

"But can you even play a guitar or sing? I always thought—"

"You kidding, I can't sing any better than when old lady McMertle tossed me out of music class in ninth grade. And, as far as playing guitar, I don't know the first thing. That's the beauty of this gig. All I gotta do is show up and look the part. All these chicks rub up against me while they're having their picture taken with me. Matter of fact, that's kind of where you come in."

"Me?"

"Yeah, I figured Bono probably doesn't go any-where without security, you know how stars are. So, of course, your name immediately popped into my thick skull. Who better to provide security than my close per-sonal private detective friend, Dev Haskell?" he said and extended his arms like he was presenting me on stage. "You know, maybe you could drive, too, since I sort of got my license taken away."

"Your license was taken away?"

"Kind of blew over the limit, by about half a point. In fact, I gotta find an attorney for my court appearance in a couple of weeks."

"I might be able to help you there. My office mate is Mr. DUI in this town."

"He's been caught?"

"What? No, he represents people. He's an attorney. He was with the city a few years back, before he opened up a private practice. Like I said, we share an office. Louie Laufen is his name."

"You kidding? Someone mentioned him to me. Yeah, yeah, I'd like to meet him."

At that point, the door opened, and an attractive woman in a white lab coat stepped into the room. She looked like she might have been Latino. She had brown eyes, her dark hair was pulled into a tight bun on the back of her head, and her name tag read Martina. She carried a small chrome tray, fortunately with a white towel over it, so I couldn't see any needles.

"Mister Winkler?" she said.

Wink nodded and raised his hand.

She stared for a long moment before she said, "Has anyone ever told you, you look exactly like Bono?"

"See," Wink said, suddenly with an accent. "Yes, ma'am, actually, that's me, Winkler is just the name I use to avoid crowds. Say, you know what, after we're done here. How about you take a picture with me, tell your friends I was in town and came in for some touch-up."

"Oh, really," she sort of giggled. "If you let me take a couple of pictures of you, we'll put it up on our web site. I'll even give you a discount."

"I'd love it," Wink said.

Seven

I waited out in the hall while Wink, aka Bono, underwent his piercing. I was leaning against the wall next to one of the framed black and white photos. This particular one was of a woman's flat stomach with a jewel inserted just above her navel. The image was from her shoulders to a couple of inches below her navel. Her hands were covering her breasts. The photographer had softened the image, and I stared at it for a long moment. As time passed, I studied all the framed photos along the hallway. I checked my watch. I thought it would only be about five minutes, but I'd been waiting in the hall for a little over a half-hour. How long does it take to run a needle through some guy's ear lobe?

I was about to head out to the lobby when the door suddenly opened, and Martina stepped out of the room. Her lab coat was unbuttoned. Her hair was hanging loose and messed. The moment she saw me, she blushed, folded her arms across the open lab coat, and immediately took off in the opposite direction.

I watched as she hurried down the hallway and disappeared around the corner before I stepped back into the room. Wink was sitting on the examination table. He was in the process of buckling his belt, and his face looked flushed. What looked like a black thong was on the floor beneath the table.

"Everything go okay?" I asked.

Wink smiled and said, "Amazing."

"I thought it would only take about five minutes. I had no idea it—"

"For the piercing? Yeah, that's about right." As he slid off the examination table, I noticed the two flashy stones, one in each ear. It also dawned on me that his shoes were off, and his jeans were unzipped.

"Why'd you take your shoes off. I thought . . ."

He smiled like a cat who'd just swallowed the canary. "Full exam," he said. "Her brush with fame."

"What?"

"I'm telling you man, it's unreal. She took some pictures of us, then a couple of me with these stones in my ears, and left with a big smile."

"She looked more embarrassed than anything else."

"Okay, so I'm the one with the big smile, works for me. Plus, I got these stones as a freebie, little extra thank you thrown in, you might say."

"Are they diamonds?"

"They look it, don't they? No, I guess they're that cubic zirconia stuff, but hey, the piercing, these stones, and some very personal attention from Painful Pleasure's Martina, all for just a couple of pictures with me. Everyone leaves happy, or, well, at least, I do. Come on, I gotta take a couple of pictures out in the lobby. After that, if you've got time, we can grab some lunch. I seem to have worked up an appetite."

With that, Wink headed out the door, and I followed him down the hall. As we entered the lobby, the conversational hum came to a dead stop, and everyone stared. He approached the receptionist and said in his fake accent, "I'm all taken care of, lassie. Now, Martina said she was going to give you a call about taking some photos and—"

"I just got off the phone with her. We'd like to take a couple of shots at the counter here and maybe sitting in one of the chairs. Hey," she said, looking at me. "Would you mind taking the pictures?" She held out her cellphone.

"Be happy to, as long as you set it, up so all I have to do is push a button."

She quickly had both thumbs flying across the cell, and, after a few seconds, she handed the phone to me. "Just push that white button. Maybe get a couple of Bono talking to me here at the reception desk. By the way, my name's Christine," she said to Wink.

He didn't bother to mention his name, but then why would he? She thought he was Bono. He leaned against the counter while she picked up the receiver on the desk phone and pretended to be talking. I took four pictures.

"Good, now a couple more where we're just talking," she said.

I took another four, plus two more, as she adjusted her pose ever so slightly.

"Maybe one or two just standing here," she said as she stood up from behind the counter and moved in close to Wink, very close. "Maybe put your arm around me, you know like you're thinking of asking me out."

Wink drew her in closer, and she rested her head on his shoulder.

"Okay, let's get some of you sitting here in the lobby. Can we use your chair for a moment?" she said to a guy who sort of reluctantly stood up. Wink sat down between two other women, early twenties type. They both leaned in toward him.

"Maybe back up a little so we can see, Bono, girls. Yeah, okay. Hold it," she said as I took two more photos. When I finished, Wink started to get out of the chair. Christine stepped over and quickly climbed onto his lap, wrapped both arms around him, pushed his head against her chest, and held it there.

I took three more photos.

"Maybe a couple more," she said.

I took another four then said, "Hey, Bono, we'd better get going. You've got that gig at the recording studio."

Christine slowly climbed off Wink's lap then hurried over to the receptionist counter. We took a half step toward the door, and she said, "Wait a sec, here's my card if you need anything or just want to call." She handed the card to Wink, then whispered, "I wrote my number on the back."

Eight

We were sitting on bar stools in Shamrock's, at one of the taller tables near the front door. Just as our lunch was delivered I said, "What do I think? I think it's unbelievable, it's absolutely nuts."

The waitress was blonde, pretty, maybe late twenties with a tattoo on her right forearm, a heart with two pink roses above and below it. The roses looked real like a person could literally pick them up.

She'd just set our lunches down in front of us. "Will there be anything else?"

"No, I think we're good," I said.

"How about a beer, or a glass of wine? Oh, sorry, I know you don't drink wine. I mean, that's what I read somewhere. Maybe a Coke?" she said, staring at Wink.

"I'd like something, but it's not on the menu," Wink said, as he leaned closer and stared into her eyes.

I rolled my eyes, an idiot guy line, if ever there was one.

"You'd be surprised what's available," she said, placing an index finger on his chest, she started moving it around in a little circle, and didn't so much as blink.

"Excuse me. I'm Bono's security, and I think we'd just like to eat lunch."

"Could be something for the both of you," she said to me, only now she wasn't smiling.

"Tell you what, you know what I'd like?" Wink said. "If you have a cellphone, I'd love to take my picture with you. Would you do that? My security guy can take the picture. He does it all the time. Surprisingly, he's pretty good."

She quickly reached into her back pocket, jabbed her cellphone at me and cuddled up next to Wink, cheek to cheek. I took three photos and set the cellphone back on the table, signaling my bourbon bacon cheeseburger was getting cold. She stayed glued to Wink for another long moment before she finally stood up.

"Call me if you want anything. Anything at all," she said, then picked up her phone and left.

"Hey, you want a beer or something? This lunch is on me?" Wink said.

"Thanks, but I better not."

"You sure, they probably won't charge us."

"You're kidding?"

"No, man, you've seen how it is. I mean, it's crazy, but I'll take it."

A family of four suddenly came up to the table. The kids, a boy and a girl, were about the same height as the table, definitely brother and sister. "Excuse me, sorry to interrupt, but would you mind if we took a picture with you?" the mom said. I pegged her at about thirty-five, the kids maybe five or six, and her husband as disgusted.

To his credit, Wink hopped off his stool, bent down, and put his arms around the kids. The mom got behind him, wrapped her arms around his neck, and rested her head on his shoulder.

"Sure you're ready, Cindy?" her husband asked and shook his head. He took two pictures and said, "Thanks a lot, sorry to interrupt. One of us is a huge fan." He nodded at his wife.

"Mom, can we go, please?" the little boy said, which made me and his father laugh.

Four more people, two women and a younger couple interrupted our fifteen-minute lunch to take pictures. That was on top of the hovering blonde waitress who stopped back to check if, "Everything was okay," a half dozen different times.

The last time she checked, I said, "Yeah, it's fine. I think if you could just bring the bill, I've got to get Bono to a practice gig. Where are you Friday night, Bono?"

"I'll be at Psycho Shelia's. I want to check out a band called U and Me. They're playing all my songs. Maybe we'll see you there."

She grinned, nodded aggressively, and said, "I'll be right back with the bill."

"There you go, taking pictures with everyone, including the waitress, and you're still paying," I said.

Wink shrugged and said, "You win some, you lose some."

The waitress was back a moment later and slid the bill in front of me. "It's been a real pleasure to serve you," she said to Wink. She slid a piece of paper across the table to him, leaned over, whispered something in his ear and gave him a lingering kiss on the cheek.

I looked at the bill. It only had my sandwich, fries and coke. I pulled fifteen bucks from my wallet, placed it on top of the bill. "Come on, Bono, let's get you to that recording gig."

The waitress escorted us to the door. "Bye, bye, don't forget, anything you want," she called and waved as we headed down the street.

Nine

As we settled into my Jeep, I said, "God. What exactly did she mean by, 'Don't forget'?"

"Just reminding me, she gets off at eight and was going to take a bubble bath."

"What?"

"I'm not kidding. Here's her phone number," he said and held out the note she had given him. It was written on a length of paper tape torn from an adding machine, but sure enough, there was her phone number and below that the words, "Bubble Bath!" written in capital letters.

"You gonna go?"

"Nah, I showered this morning."

I shot a look his way until traffic cleared, and I merged back on to West Seventh Street. "Where do you want me to drop you?"

"Might as well take me home, I got stuff to do this afternoon."

"Be happy to, but since I haven't seen you for close to fifteen years, maybe you could tell me where you live."

"Oh, yeah, right. I'm in my folks' place, on St. Paul Avenue."

"You're living with your folks?"

He looked at me, "Really? They'd want to kill me, and the two of them would drive me crazy. They moved into a Florida condo about ten years ago. I think the day after the old man retired. They're up here on holidays and stay with me, but after about forty-eight hours, they can't wait to get back to Florida."

"Forty-eight hours with you, who can blame them."

"Works both ways, man. I love 'em dearly, but my mom is never short of directions."

"You got plans for the rest of the day?"

"Yeah, if you can believe it, I'm studying up on Bono, and I gotta memorize some of his songs."

"Mind if I mention something?"

"Not a problem, shoot."

"Well Bono, and the whole band, I think, they're all from Dublin. Any of these women ever mention that? You know, like why the hell are you talking in that goofy accent?"

"You know, it's weird. Soon as they hear me talk, I think they probably know I'm not really him, but they still want a couple of pictures taken, and somewhere along the way they sort of convince themselves it doesn't really matter, they'd like to ride me. That Martina at Painful Pleasures was the perfect example."

"Yeah, that was more than a little crazy. I guess that sort of thing doesn't happen every day."

"Every day?" he said and smiled. "Try every hour, believe me, I'd be exhausted. Probably have to call 911 by noon, just to resuscitate me."

"Friday night, what time you want me to pick you up?" I said, changing the subject.

The band doesn't start playing at Psycho Shelia's until nine-thirty. Why don't you swing by, so I can make a grand entrance around ten? Can you dress like those high buck security guys?"

"I'll be sure to do that," I said as I pulled in front of his place. It looked pretty much the same as what I remembered. A 1950's three-bedroom rambler. The boulevard trees were a little larger and the grass needed cutting. The house was more or less the same color, but faded and peeling in spots. Wink's dad would never have allowed that to happen.

"See you Friday night," he said, as he climbed out of the Jeep and headed into his house. I drove back to the office.

Ten

I'd just settled into my office chair. I was actually sitting on a pillow, just to provide some added comfort after the previous night's assault from Heidi. As if on cue, my phone rang.

"Haskell Investigations."

"Well, if you answered, I guess you survived," Heidi said and laughed.

"Mmm-mmm, barely. It's gonna take some time to recover, darling."

"Oh, you big baby. Hey, I just wanted to thank you for taking the time to listen to me. I just don't know what it is about me that men don't like."

"Well, I told you last night. Although after the better part of two bottles of wine, you probably don't remember."

"You were here last night?" she said, then followed up with, "Okay, sorry, but I just couldn't resist. Remind me what you said."

"I told you the same thing I've told you before. The advice you never seem to listen to. I don't think it's you. I think it's the sort of guy you're attracted to."

"Well, I like you."

"Yeah, but that's different. The guys you aggressively go after are pretty much all professional, doctors, lawyers, that guy in the governor's office—"

"He was a real jerk."

"Heidi, no offense, but they're all real jerks. This latest one, Jon."

"Actually, he prefers to be called Jonathan."

"Yeah, exactly, what a pain in the ass. Hey, I prefer to be called super stud, but a lot of folks just call me Dev."

"You're not making any sense."

"Only 'cause you're not paying attention, Heidi. These guys that you date and then end up broken-hearted over, they've all got a superior attitude. They may be successful at what they do, but we both know there's more to life than that. This last guy, Jonny—"

"Jonathan, Dev."

"See, there you go, the guy lied to you, cheated on his wife, he's got two kids, and for some reason, you're correcting me about his name. You should be calling him asshole, or dip shit or something. But at some level, you're still impressed enough that you feel the need to correct me. No offense, but you have to sort of wonder if you were the first time he cheated on his wife, or is it his modus operandi."

"Whoa, listen to you using big words. Mmm-mmm, sexy. All of a sudden, I want you over here."

"Yeah, right, give me a couple of days to recover before I venture back into your bedroom. Look, all I'm saying is, it's never fun having a relationship go south, but maybe it doesn't mean you're not right. Maybe it's just that you're attracted to high profile jerks, with the exception of me, of course."

"I wouldn't call you high profile."

"But you'd call me a jerk?"

"I regularly call you something far worse than a jerk."

"Now, you're using your head."

"Thanks, Dev," she said, sounding a lot happier, all of sudden. "I'll catch you later."

Eleven

The guard said, "Gentlemen review this inventory list you filled out when you joined us thirty days ago. Sign your name at the bottom of the form stating everything has been returned to you. This will complete your release process, and once signed, you're free to go."

Clarence tore open the manila envelope, checked his wallet to make sure the seven dollars was still in there before he signed the form and shoved it back across the Formica counter.

Delton pulled the car keys and his wallet from the envelope and shoved them into his pocket. He scribbled a capital 'D,' drew a line that ran off the edge of the form, and slid it across the counter.

The guard flashed a nanosecond smile that suggested he'd be seeing them again, then pressed a button beneath the counter, and the steel door on the far side of the room clicked open.

Delton hurried past his brother, Clarence, and out the door. Their car, a rusted blue, Olds 88, sat in a far corner of the parking lot. "I'll drive," Delton said, unlocking the passenger door and sliding across the front seat until he was behind the wheel.

"What's the rush, man? It's not like we have to be anywhere."

"Were you paying attention to the plans we discussed? Remember the newspaper story? He's in town and checking out some band at Psycho Shelia's on Friday night. We gotta be there early, so we can get in the place. Probably gotta pay a cover charge, so I was just thinking it might be nice if we had some cash."

"Be lots of women there. After thirty days in that damn workhouse I wouldn't mind a little action."

"Then, let's get going," Delton said. He cranked the ignition for a good fifteen seconds before a blue cloud of exhaust exploded from the tailpipe, and the engine groaned to life.

Twelve

Friday night arrived, and I pulled in front of Wink's a little before nine. The porch light was off, but light in the living room peeked out from behind the drapes. I waited a couple of minutes, hoping he'd look out and see me. He didn't. I phoned him next, but after five rings, I got dumped into his message center.

"Hello, you've, ahh, reached Bono." He cleared his throat. "Just wanted to say I can't take your call at the moment, so leave a message and I'll try and get back to you once I finish this gig." Beep.

"Hey, Wink, it's Dev. I'm waiting out front for you," I said and hung up. After another five minutes, I finally went up to his door and rang the doorbell. I could hear music blaring from inside the house. I knocked on the door thirty seconds later. When he didn't answer, I pounded on the door, hard. I ended up going around to the back, through the gate in the picket fence, and across the small patio.

There was a set of patio doors, fortunately unlocked, and I slid the door open. Music assaulted my ears to the point where it actually hurt. I put my hands over my ears, walked through the kitchen and into the living room.

There he was, wearing the rose-colored glasses and mimicking the movements of Bono who was jumping around on the tv.

Wink was dressed exactly the same as the other day, black jeans, a black t-shirt and a black vest over the t-shirt. Tonight the vest had silver buttons and what looked like silk lapels, although I guessed the lapels were more than likely nylon.

I picked the remote up from an end table and immediately lowered the sound down from forty to zero.

"What the hell?"

"Hey, dumb shit," I said and watched as Wink jumped before he turned around. "You were in the process of destroying what was left of your hearing."

"Oh, sorry, didn't hear you come in."

"Yeah, and you didn't hear me call you, ring the doorbell, or pound on the front door."

"Oh, sorry about that, just trying to get some moves down."

"Please, promise me you're not going to sing."

"Not a problem, believe me, I won't be singing. Just thought, you know in case they get me up on stage, I could maybe give a couple of shakes or something."

"A couple of shakes? And what's with the Bono message on the phone."

He grinned, "You like it? I went on YouTube and listened to some phone message he left for a guy. Actually, I think my message sounded pretty good. I even cleared my throat like he did."

"If you say so. Hey, it's after nine, you said you wanted to be there around ten."

"Yeah, we got plenty of time." He stood back and examined me. I was dressed in a grey suit with a tie. Actually, the tie was the only one I had, and if you squeezed the thing, it played jingle bells. But it was a nondescript pattern that sort of went with the grey suit and besides, like I said, it was the only one I had.

"Hey, check this out." I slipped an earbud into my right ear. I got it on a flight out to L.A. a few months back. I pulled out a pair of sunglasses and held my hand up to the earbud like I was listening to someone talking. "How do I look?"

"Oh, man, that's perfect. You really look the part, Dev."

"Dig this," I said and put on the sunglasses. The lenses were just dark enough, so a person couldn't see where I was looking. "Plus, I got this made up, my security I.D."

I pulled a card from my pocket, the King of Hearts. I had it plastic-coated, then punched a hole in one of the corners and tied a yellow shoelace from my hockey skate through the hole so it could hang around my neck.

"Oh, man. You look like the real deal, Dev. You carrying?"

"A gun? No, bad idea bringing one into a bar. Some drunk will try and grab it thinking it would be funny, and he'll either shoot me or someone around me. We'd just be asking for trouble."

Wink nodded like that made sense and said, "What do you say? Should we head out? I'm supposed to call once we get there and they'll tell me how to get in. They're expecting a pretty big crowd."

Thirteen

Psycho Shelia's was about a fifteen-minute drive, over in the suburb of Woodbury. The place could be seen from Interstate 94 heading east. It was a two-story, white stucco building with a massive parking lot on three sides. We could hear the music from a block away, and actually, it didn't sound all that bad. When we pulled up to the building, the parking lot was jammed, and cars were parked along the street for as far as we could see. There was a line out front waiting to get into the place. A large sign mounted on three blue steel pillars rose up and towered about thirty feet above the building. The yellow sign was oval, with large black letters that advertised;

TONIGHT
U & Me Live!
With special guest appearance!

"Don't tell me, you're the special guest appearance?" I said to Wink. He was sitting in the back seat, being chauffeured around by his security detail, namely me.

"Holy shit, the women won't be able to get enough of me. That's great, come on, let's go."

"How 'bout you make your phone call first, find out how we're supposed to get into the place while I look for somewhere to park."

"Oh, yeah." Wink pulled his phone out and dialed. "Hey, it's Bono. Yeah, just pulled up in front. No. No. Just my security detail, it's just one man tonight, trying to keep a low profile. Yes. No. Yes. Sounds good, see you shortly," he said and hung up.

"We go around in back, there's a door marked for Deliveries, we just knock three times, and they'll let us in."

I drove down the street for two blocks and still couldn't find a place to park. I doubled back, drove through Psycho Shelia's parking lot, but couldn't find an open space to save my soul. As we headed out of the lot, I passed the dumpster and stopped.

"Wait here for a minute. I got an idea." I got out of the Jeep, rolled the dumpster back and forth, turning it ninety degrees until I had it positioned sideways, jutting out into the parking lot, but there was still enough space for a car to drive past. I backed the Jeep into where the dumpster had been. There was just enough room to get out of the Jeep on the driver's side, and maybe a good half-inch away from the dumpster on the passenger side.

"Slick, man. This works for me," Wink said.

I got out and had to open the rear door for him since the handle was broken, and it couldn't be opened from inside. At the corner of the building, closest to us, was the door marked for deliveries. We walked over, and I pounded on the door three times. Just as it opened, three women walked around the corner and looked at us.

"Oh, you guys, look, it's really him," one of the women shouted. They all screamed, hurried toward us just as we stepped inside, and the door closed behind us.

The guy who opened the door was maybe seventy-plus. He gave Wink a questioning look and said, "You're Bone?"

"Not quite, it's Bono," Wink said.

"Yeah, whatever. Look, the band is coming up on a break, go through that door next to the beer cases, and you can wait for them in there. I gotta get back to the bar, we're jammed." He looked at me and said, "You want to make a couple of bucks? I'll give you thirty bucks an hour if you want to pour beers. We can't keep up."

"Nah, he can't, he's my security," Wink said.

"Good luck with that," the old guy said, and we headed for the stack of beer cases.

Fourteen

We heard the band announce they were going to play one more number before the break. They played a song I didn't recognize for another fifteen minutes before they stopped and left the stage to weak applause from the packed house. Three steps from backstage led down into the room where Wink and I were waiting. As the first guy hurried down the steps, he stopped, causing the three members following behind to run into one another.

"Holy shit. Are you the guy we hired, or are you really Bono?" the first guy said.

"Tonight, I'm Bono," Wink said. "Nice to meet you guys, you sounded pretty good out there."

"Thanks, bit of a pain in the ass crowd tonight. They don't really seem to be into the gig too much." All four guys were dressed in jeans and different U2 t-shirts.

"Maybe I can get them paying a little more attention. What'd you have in mind for me?" Wink said.

Blank looks all around.

"We didn't really think of that. What'd you usually do?"

To his credit, Wink made it sound like he did a major performance every night, and this was just one more.

"What really works is when you guys go back out, start in with your number. Then, about halfway through, I'll step out on the stage, walk around a little bit, get their attention. Who's singing lead?"

"That'd be me, name's Kevin," a heavyset guy said.

"Okay, I'm going to come up next to you, and when you're singing, I'll be alongside of you mouthing the words, making it look like I'm singing. We'll work the crowd I'll maybe say a few words at the end of the song. And I mean a few words. Sound good?"

They all nodded.

Wink looked at me, "Dev, I want you off to the side, but in plain sight, pretend you're listening into your earpiece. Scan the crowd, maybe point out to us where the hot looking women are."

Kevin, the lead singer, shook his head. "I don't know, man. If there are any hotties here, we sure haven't seen them."

"I step out on that stage you guys better be ready, it's gonna go crazy," Wink said.

"Yeah, we'll see about that, Bono," one of the guys replied, and everyone laughed.

They sat on a faded blue, well-worn couch, chugging down bottles of water and not saying very much. Eventually, Kevin took his cellphone out, checked the time, and said, "Okay, a couple of minutes, and we're back out."

"Dev," Wink said. "Maybe you should go out there now and sort of scan the crowd and do the earphone thing. I'll be out a few minutes into the first number."

I stepped onto the stage with my sunglasses on and took up a position off to the side. I got a few glances, but no one paid any real attention to me. The band came out a couple of minutes later. In a crowd of two or three hundred people, maybe only a half-dozen people clapped as the band returned, probably their girlfriends and a couple of pals.

They kicked into a U2 song, the name of which escaped me. A few more heads turned. A couple of people had that look on their face that suggested their conversation had just been interrupted. It went like that for another verse, no one wandering closer than twenty feet toward the stage. The third verse kicked in, something about 'The battle's just begun,' and Wink stepped on stage.

A few people started to wander over. Wink stepped in front of the drummer, who was on a slightly raised platform and patted the base player on the shoulder. As the band broke into the chorus, he stepped up next to Kevin and mouthed the words, and suddenly the place erupted with screams and shouts. The area in front of the stage that had been empty less than fifteen seconds before was suddenly filled by screaming women with their hands stretched out.

Two guys, one with a heavy-duty news camera and the other carrying a long-handled microphone with a fuzzy grey cover suddenly appeared. They stood up against the stage and focused on Wink.

Wink did a quick pass back and forth along the front of the stage, giving all sorts of women a high five. The ones closest to the stage reached out to touch him, grabbed at his shoes, and blew kisses. Everyone in the band wore wide eyes and large grins as the crowd continued to scream and go crazy.

When they finished the song, Kevin stepped back up to the microphone and said, "How 'bout a little round of applause for our special guest." He stepped back and extended a hand toward Wink.

"Thank you, lads and lassies," Wink said in a dreadful accent, but nobody seemed to mind. Something pink flew out of the crowd, bounded off of Wink's chest, then dropped to the floor. He reached down and picked up a small pink thong, waved it over his head, and shouted, "Thanks, darling."

Not that anyone could hear him. The screams rose to an even higher decibel level. The band struck up a new song, and Wink mouthed the words with Kevin. Nodding at him as if to say, "Keep it up, you're doing fine." Another thong landed on stage.

Wink pretended to sing three more songs, making a pass back and forth across the stage and giving high fives to a few hundred women along the way with every song. At one point, he got the entire place clapping more or less to the beat.

I had to follow him across the stage, stopping various women from climbing up or pulling him off and into the crowd. One of the women jumped up and pinched my ass. I turned around and shouted, "I'll give you a half-hour to stop that."

She blew me a kiss.

We were back in the break room after the last number. The band was all smiles, we were all drenched in sweat, and we couldn't hear what anyone was saying because out in front of the stage the crowd was chanting, "Bono, Bono, Bono . . ."

Kevin held up his hands, indicating playing a guitar, and mouthed the words encore. They started to head back on stage then turned as one and looked at Wink.

He held up two fingers and shouted, "Second verse."

They nodded, went back onstage to thunderous applause and screams, and started to play. Wink and I headed out on the second verse. It was more of the same, and then the song ended, the lights dimmed, and we escaped back into the break room.

Fifteen

Kevin slapped everyone's hands and said, "Did you catch that shit? We're in the big leagues," We were all drenched in sweat and had cans of beer in our hands from a micro-brewery named Able Brewing. The drummer, I'd already forgotten his name, pulled a light blue thong from his pocket, stretched it along his index finger, and shot it at Kevin.

"Yeah, and where did that come from, the thongs, incredible."

The door leading out to the stage suddenly opened, and three women hurried in. The woman in the lead almost fell down the three stairs into the room.

"Hey, what the . . ."

"Oh, wow, sorry, we were sort of wondering if we could get an autograph," she said as she pulled herself back on her feet.

They were all attractive if you didn't mind them drenched in sweat. Two of them wore shorts. The third had a short skirt. They all wore U2 t-shirts.

"We had no idea, I mean, this was just so cool."

"How 'bout a beer, darlings?" Wink said, attempting another dreadful sounding accent.

Kevin, the lead in the band, looked about to say something, but Wink caught his attention.

"Let's all get in nice and close. Ladies," Wink nodded at a blue plastic cooler on the floor. "Help yourselves to a beer, then Dev, if you'd take our picture. Now, if you're going to be posting these photos, do me a favor and tell everyone tonight's band is called 'U and Me'," he said and spelled it out to them.

They all nodded as one of the band members handed them a beer.

"Okay," Wink said. "Everyone crowd in."

The women closed in on Wink, he wrapped his arms around them, and I took two photos on each of the three cell phones.

"Can we get an autograph?"

"You can if you've got a pen."

She gave a disappointed scowl, then Kevin said, "I got one in my case, hang on."

He opened his guitar case, pulled out a pen, and handed it to her. She had Wink sign her pink cellphone case. Another pulled what looked like a store receipt from a back pocket, and Wink signed that. Actually, to be precise, he forged Bono's signature.

"Okay, my turn," the woman in the short skirt said. She stepped forward and pulled up her U2 t-shirt exposing a flesh-colored bra. "If you could write me a little note and sign it, that would be great."

"I'll write you a long letter if you keep this shirt pulled up."

When he was done, the drummer said, "That wasn't your thong was it, that blue one over there on the couch?"

She glanced over and shook her head. "No, mine was red, and it didn't make it onto the stage."

"Thank you, ladies, come on, let me show you out the secret door over here," I said and ushered them out the door we'd first entered.

"Thanks," they all shouted as they exited the room.

I looked at one of the band members and said, "See if you can lock that door off the stage. It'd be nice to get a break from all the craziness."

"I gotta tell you, this has been a first for us," Kevin said, looking around at the other band members. They were all nodding. "That was just really cool. You know we got another gig here tomorrow night. You interested? Pay both of you double."

Sixteen

They were seated in a far corner of Psycho Shelia's bar. Actually, Delton was seated, Clarence had been standing since they arrived almost six and a half hours earlier. With the band finally finished, the place had more or less emptied out in fifteen minutes.

"So, what'd you think," Delton said.

"Hard to hear with all them broads screaming and shit. You know me, I'm more partial to country-western anyway, give me Tim McGraw, Kenny Chesney, Carrie Under—"

"Clarence, you paying attention? I meant Bono. You pick up on anything?"

"Yeah, he ain't all that tall."

Delton took a deep breath and exhaled. "I meant he had security, that dude with the sun-glasses in that suit. We're going to have to deal with him. They made that announcement they're gonna be back here tomorrow night, it'll be perfect."

"Dealing with that security fella, that could be fun," Clarence said and drained his glass.

Delton shook his head. "We need to take him out, not kill him. Just get him out of our way, try not to attract attention, once we get rid of the security problem we grab that Bono dude and head up to the cabin and get ready for a lifetime of cold beer and pretty women."

"Where we going to grab him?"

"Here."

"What?"

"Yeah, here. Think about it. They'll sit around in some fancy room backstage drinking fancy drinks. Place is probably full of naked women until everyone clears out. Then, once it's safe, they'll head out. In a way, it makes the setup perfect for us. They won't be expecting anything. We'll just grab Bono, throw him in the car, and away we go."

"You sure that's gonna work."

Delton nodded and said, "Yeah, cause we're gonna check it out tonight. Come on, let's wait for 'em out in the parking lot."

Seventeen

It was almost three in the morning, and we'd finally been able to sneak into my Jeep. We had to wait a good couple of hours before the crowd thinned out and we could sneak out the rear door. Fortunately, just about anyone left was milling around the front of Psycho Shelia's waiting to catch a glimpse of the big star. "Oh, man, can you dig that? A couple hundred bucks," Wink said.

Wink had to duck down onto the floor of the back seat before we slowly inched our way through the hard-core crowd still out front. God only knew how long they'd remain hanging around waiting to catch a glimpse. I never noticed the rusted blue, Olds 88 in the far corner of the parking lot.

"So you're going to do it, the gig with them tomorrow night," I said to Wink on the floor of the back seat.

"Well, yeah, they said they'd pay me double. Two hundred bucks to have women pull there tops up and expose themselves. Count me in."

"When did someone do that?"

"Well, I mean they could, Dev. You saw the thongs on stage, didn't you? And don't forget the bra I autographed."

"Yeah, I guess. Now that you mention it. Hey, I'm about to pull onto the freeway, you can get up off the floor?"

"Oh, yeah, thanks. You're gonna be coming with me tomorrow night, aren't you?"

"Ahh, I don't know, Wink. I mean, don't get me wrong, it was an interesting experience and all, but one night of this was probably enough for me. I mean, I get it, women throwing their underwear at you and everything, but need I point out, at the end of the night I'm still driving home with you, and you're still riding home with me."

"I suppose I should have just taken off with those three who came into the dressing room," he said as he climbed up off the back floor and onto the seat.

"Yeah, sure, that would have worked. Soon as they came to their senses and realized they had a look-a-like in the car who couldn't sing to save his soul, they'd kick you out in the middle of nowhere."

"Yeah, maybe, or maybe they would have brought me home and given themselves a night to remember."

"Really, you think that was what was going to happen?"

"Hey, just sayin' it could have. You never know, man."

"Yeah, you got that part right, you never know."

"Come on, do another night with me. It'll be fun. They said they'd pay you. Tell me the truth, now, you enjoyed yourself, right?"

"Yeah, I enjoyed myself watching you. I have to admit. The whole thing is nothing short of amazing."

"You know, Dev, I'm thinking I could turn this into some kind of whole new business. Going around doing grand openings for stores, maybe throwing the first pitch at a world series game. Just think if I set up a little studio and all sorts of chicks could come in and have their picture taken with me. I mean, would that be cool or what?"

"I'm not sure cool is the term you're looking for, more like crazy, but certainly not cool."

"That's okay, man. You want to rain on the parade, go ahead, be my guest. Apparently, you must have been on a different stage than I was because I saw women pushing each other out of the way just to be able to say they touched me. I saw women throwing their thongs up onto the stage at me. You heard that one chick. She was disappointed because hers didn't make it onto the stage. God, the woman pulls up her t-shirt so I'll autograph her bra when was the last time that happened to you?"

"Course all of this happened because they thought you were someone else, Wink. Pardon me if I missed it along the way, but with my foggy memory, I can't recall you autographing anything with the name Luther Winkler, or am I forgetting something."

"Go ahead, man, keep raining on the parade."

"I got a better idea," I said as we pulled up in front of Wink's place. "Get the hell out of my car, this is your house."

"Thanks for the ride, Dev. It was great to spend a crazy night with you and good to catch up after all this time. You sure I can't talk you into tomorrow night?"

"Tell you what, Wink, let me sleep on it, and I'll call you in the morning."

"Okay, thanks, I appreciate it. Hey, open the door for me, will you, so I can get out of here."

Eighteen

Louie must have had a court appearance because it was after eleven, and he still hadn't been in the office. I was scanning the empty sidewalks and apartments across the street with the binoculars, not seeing a soul. It was over ninety degrees and rising, so the temperature might have had something to do with the lack of subjects to watch.

My phone rang just as a redheaded woman in a skimpy yellow outfit came around the corner and stood at the bus stop. I was double tasking, admiring her outfit through the binoculars while listening to the phone ring. I answered after the third ring.

"Haskell Investigations."

"Well, it's nice to know at least you're still alive."

"Oh, hi, Sassy, I was just about to call you," I lied. "How are things?"

"Really? You were going to call me?"

I couldn't tell if she was kidding or not.

"What's up?"

"Well, I'm feeling insecure if you must know."

I did not want to sit in a chair out in the hallway in front of her penthouse, no matter what she paid.

"The police didn't offer to come over?"

"They took down my information again. But no, to answer your question. They did not offer to come over and to tell you the truth, I've driven past the building a number of times, and I've been checking the lobby almost every hour, but no one seems to be keeping an eye on things."

Yeah, like the cops have time to waste doing that. "Remember, I said they would be out of uniform, working undercover."

"Mmm-mmm, I'm not so sure. I was thinking maybe you should come over tonight."

"Tonight? Oh, gee, I wish I could, but I'm working security tonight, sorry. Unfortunately, I'll be booked until sometime after two."

"Sometime after two? What parking lot is open that late?"

"This may come as a surprise, but I'm not working parking lot security. Actually, I'm providing security for Bono."

"Bono? So that really was you on stage with him last night? I saw a fifteen-second post on YouTube. I just didn't think it was you, must have been the suit that threw me off."

"Yeah, that was me. YouTube? Huh, interesting. I'll have to check it out. I was with him last night, and I'm covering him again tonight. You can imagine the crazy fans he's got to deal with. It's absolutely wild." I conjured up an image of gorgeous Martina at Painful Pleasures as she blushed in her unbuttoned lab coat exiting the room.

"Dev, you have to introduce me. I'm his biggest fan."

"Oh, gee, I'd love to, Sassy. Unfortunately, a clause in my contract prevents me from introducing him to anyone. I'm hired to keep people away from him, or, well at least keep them at a safe distance. I'm sure you understand."

"How long is he in town for?"

"I'm not even sure. As far as I know, tonight might be his last night. I think he's hopping on a flight right after the gig."

"No, no, it can't be. I have to meet him. Dev, listen, I'll make this worth your while."

"Thanks, Sassy, but I don't think there's much I can—"

"No, Dev, you're not listening. I mean, really worth your while."

"Sassy, I'm pretty sure he won't let—"

"Dev, are you listening? I'm not offering to pay you, at least not money. I'm talking about something you've always dreamed about. Something you've always wanted."

"You mean—"

"Oh, yes, and a lot more. Benefits, baby, real benefits. Believe me, I'm very good. All my husbands said so. Wilder than you ever imagined. You know what I'm wearing right now?"

I turned away from the redhead at that bus stop and set the binoculars on my desk.

"N-n-no."

"Just a smile. I couldn't wait to get undressed and call you."

I knew she was talking absolute bullshit, and I didn't care.

"I need to meet Bono. I know you can arrange that. Why not think about how you're going to accomplish that and then think about joining me tonight after he's finished with his gig."

"Tonight?"

"Yes, well, provided I can wait that long. I just might have to start without you. What do you say?"

"Okay, yeah, I mean, I'll be there. You know, Bono might be giving an interview or something. What if he can't make it tonight?"

"Tonight, Dev, before he leaves town. I mean it. I'm counting on you. I'm going to go out now to buy a very skimpy outfit just for the occasion. You just call me and tell me where and when."

"Yeah, okay, I think I can do that."

"I know you can. Oh, and Dev?"

"Yeah?'

"Better rest up, honey, you're going to need it."

Nineteen

I phoned Wink and ended up leaving a message. He called me back later that afternoon.

"Haskell Investigations."

"Hey, sorry I missed your call, I had the music on and was practicing my moves."

"Your Bono moves?"

"Yeah. Now, tell me you're going to make it tonight."

"Yeah, I think I might."

"You think you might?"

"Well, see, I got a bit of a complication."

"What kind of complication?"

"Who was the hottest girl in high school?"

"Who? What do you mean, who? Hands down, Sassy Aronson. Remember, I asked her out about a million times only she always turned me down. Then, she got that stupid thug boyfriend after me. What's his name?"

"Jerry Baker?"

"Yeah, the bastard's probably in prison by now."

"Actually, that's where he sends people. He's a judge."

"A judge? You gotta be kidding me."

"No, apparently, he's presided over all three of her divorces."

"She's been divorced three times? Hey, what does this have to do with my gig tonight?"

"She wants to meet you?"

"Meet me? She couldn't stand me. You're talking about the blonde girl who was drop-dead gorgeous and a real pain in the ass, right? She didn't have time for me, well, and for that matter, she didn't have time for you either, or any of us come to think about it."

"Yeah, she called me to guard her penthouse, and I told her I was working security for you."

"For me?"

"Well, actually, I didn't mention you directly. I just told her I was doing security for Bono tonight."

"What'd she say."

"She basically told me she'd do anything to meet you," I said, figuring there was no point in going into detail.

"So, she bought it?"

"Yeah, said she was counting on me to line it up, and she was going out to buy a skimpy outfit."

"Be a shame to disappoint her."

"Yeah, that was my thought, too. Here's the deal, though, you gotta stay true Bono all night. Don't let on. I'm going to tell her to meet us at Psycho Shelia's at like six. We get there early, you can talk to her in the room behind the stage. But you gotta stay in the Bono role all night, okay?"

"Okay? You kidding? I'm hanging up the phone, and I'm gonna practice my accent. Right now."

"Okay, I'll pick you up at 5:30. I'll tell her to knock on that door three times, and we'll let that owner guy know, so he lets her in."

"Think he will?"

"You hear him last night, he didn't have enough bartenders, based on the crowd you're bringing in, he'll do anything you want. But you gotta promise me, Wink, you're gonna be Bono all night."

"Relax, I got it man. Oh, I mean, matey," he said.

I phoned Sassy back and left a message.

"Hi Sassy, Dev. I cleared it with Bono, he'll meet you for a minute, but he's really busy. Be at Psycho Shelia's a little after six. There's a back door marked for Deliveries, knock three times on the door, and they'll let you in. Just you. If there's anyone else with you, they won't let you in and don't tell anyone. Call me, so I know you got this message."

I'd barely disconnected when my phone rang.

"Haskell Invest—"

"Oh, Dev, thank you, thank you, thank you."

"Oh. So you got my message."

"Yes, and I can't thank you enough. I'm so excited."

"Well, just remember our deal, Sassy."

"Oh relax, yeah, yeah, of course. Say, do you think Bono would like to maybe join—"

"Actually, no, he's not into that."

"He's gay?"

"No, but he's really, you know, loyal to his wife, and if you mention anything like that to him, he'll have you tossed out, so don't say anything."

"Okay, yeah, thanks for the warning. Psycho Shelia's?"

"Right, you know it? It's out in Woodbury, just along I-94."

"Believe me, I'll find it. Oh, I can't thank you enough."

"Okay, see you at six, and remember our deal."

"I won't forget, Dev, Thank you, thank you, thank you," she said and disconnected.

"Woo-hoo-hoo, Sassy Aronson."

Twenty

I was fifteen minutes early and dressed in the same grey suit and Christmas tie from last night when I pulled up in front of Wink's house. He was already watching out the front window. He had hurried out onto the front stoop and was locking the door before I came to a stop. He ran to the car and opened the front passenger door. "Hey, Dev, how's it going?"

"Wink, climb into the back, so it looks like you're being chauffeured around."

"What? Oh, yeah, yeah. Thanks, man." He slammed the door, climbed into the back seat, and closed the door behind him.

A moment later, I was engulfed by a cloud of aftershave that almost made my eyes water. I glanced at him in the rearview mirror. He was in essentially the same outfit as the night before. The glasses, black jeans, and the vest with the silver buttons over the black t-shirt.

He grinned back at me, raised his eyebrows, and said, "Sassy Aronson."

"Yeah, she's going to be there around six, at least, that's what she told me."

"Good, that'll give me some time to, ahem, get caught up with her," Wink said.

I turned to look at him in the back seat. "Just remember man, the deal is you're going to be Bono the entire night. You're not going to step out of character. She doesn't know it's you, so don't tell her. It'll only screw things up for both of us."

"Relax, man, I even called Kevin and told him. They'll all be on board. Remember those guys with the camera and microphone last night? I guess one of the stations ran a news blurb on the morning and noon news, probably rerunning it tonight as I speak. They bought into it, hook, line and sinker. Led with it this morning, I watched the thing on YouTube a half dozen times. They opened with the line, 'Big name in our home town.' Kevin sent me a text just a bit ago. I guess they already have folks filling up the parking lot, so we should get our ass over there. It's going to be crazier than last night. I bet they raise the price at the door."

"Then you really better stay in character, they find out you're you, a lot of those folks won't be too happy."

"Hmmm, I didn't think of that, but amazingly, you're probably right. Come on, let's get over there, man," Wink said, then settled in and buckled up.

Traffic seemed okay until about a mile from the exit ramp to Psycho Shelia's where it began to back up.

"Hey, Wink, check this out."

"Oh, man, what is it an accident up ahead?"

"No, I think these folks are going to see, Bono, man. Hey, do me a favor, get down on the floor. Some idiot sees you they're liable to tail us or do something stupid."

"You think?"

"I know, man. Come on, get down on the floor, or we're never going to get into the place."

Wink slid down onto the floor as I bypassed the line of cars waiting to take a right at the top of the ramp. I drove up onto the curb and slowly proceeded up the exit ramp with my lefthand blinker on. Fortunately, there was no oncoming traffic at the top of the ramp. I made a quick right turn, drove on the wrong side of the road for a half-block, and turned onto the frontage road.

There was a line of cars waiting to get into Psycho Shelia's parking lot. Three guys wearing green high visibility vests stood at the entrance collecting a ten dollar parking fee.

"Holy shit."

"What is it?" Wink called from the floor of the back seat.

"Stay down man it's a mess. Hang on." I said. I made a sharp right up over the curb and across Psycho Shelia's front lawn headed toward the parking lot. One of the high visibility vest guys, the largest of the three, picked up a baseball bat leaning against the building and slammed it onto the top of my hood.

"What the hell do you think you're doing, mother—"

I lowered my window and waved him over to my side. He wound up like he was going to slam the bat into my windshield.

"Wait, wait, don't man. I got Bono in here. We're trying to sneak in."

Fortunately, he put down the bat, looked more than a little confused, and said, "What?"

"Check out the back seat, man. I got Bono in here. We're trying to get in without creating a major scene. Can you let us through?"

He peeked over my shoulder and looked down at Wink sitting on the floor. Wink smiled and gave a little wave.

"Oh, yeah, man. Listen, hang on just a minute, and we'll get you in. Let me make a call." He pulled out his cell, pushed two buttons, and a moment later said, "Arty, I got your main man out here. No, dude, for real. I'm going to walk him back, get by the back door and be ready to let him in so he doesn't have to stand out here or you're gonna have a real mess on your hands. Yeah. Yeah. About ninety seconds."

He yelled at the two other guys in the high vis-vests. "Hey, guys, shut down while I get this car back there. It'll just take a minute."

"You kidding me?" one of the guys yelled.

"Just do it man," he said. He moved the orange and white barrier a couple of feet to the side so I could pull into the parking lot, then ran in front of us and directed us up to a spot right against the back of the building. He held his hand up, signaling us to remain in the car then knocked on the door marked Deliveries. The door opened a moment later, and the crabby old guy owner waved us out of the car.

The lot was already jammed, and they were still letting cars in. People were driving over the grass medians and parking in the lots on either side and behind Psycho Shelia's. A steady stream of people were walking towards the front of the building. They gave us a casual glance but kept moving.

"Wink, you stay in the car until I open the door for you, got it?"

"Dev, is this cool or what?"

"It's an absolute nightmare is what it is. Once you're out of the car, just get your ass inside. Got it?"

"Yeah, yeah, relax, I'm cool, dude."

I climbed out, hurried around the back of the car, and opened the door. "Come on, man, let's go."

"Oh, man, can you dig this?" Wink said as he stepped out and glanced around.

"Oh, my god, it's him. There he is," a woman screamed to her girlfriends no more than fifteen feet off to the side.

"Oi, lassie, would you—"

I yanked Wink by the arm, hard, and hurried him in through the back door before they could make it over to us. The crabby old guy slammed the door closed once we were inside. A second or two later, all sorts of pounding and screaming came from the other side.

"Did you catch that?" Wink half-shouted and grinned

"Man, don't do that. Don't call 'em over," I said.

"I don't know what it is, but you certainly seem to be able to attract them," the owner said and shook his head.

Twenty-one

They'd been in the back of Psycho Shelia's parking lot for the better part of two hours, leaning against the hood of their Olds 88 sipping beers. Just now, they were watching the half dozen women pounding on the delivery door trying to get in. "Oh, you see that shit? This is going to be a cakewalk," Delton said.

"I don't know man, lots of people. It's going to be tough grabbing him and getting our asses out of here," Clarence said and took a healthy sip.

"Relax, we're gonna be just fine. We're in no rush. When the time is right, we'll grab him. In the meantime, once the music starts and all these fools go inside, we'll just make sure they can't get away in that car."

"Yeah, about that Jeep. Don't these big-name rock stars usually travel around in stretch limos with a bunch of good looking women?"

"You're still not catching on, Clarence. You see any advertising for this gig? Hell, the sign out front doesn't even mention his name. It's like a secret kind of star deal. Probably trying out some new songs and shit. Hell, if it weren't for that news station this noon, none of these folks would even be here. They're trying to keep it all nice and quiet, see? That's why they show up in that half-ass Jeep. What famous dude wants to be seen in that piece of shit? Just makes it that much easier for us. Is all. We'll just sit back and take it easy, grab another beer or two and wait until it's our turn to make the headlines. Matter of fact, why don't you make yourself useful for a change and grab me another one?" Delton said. He crumpled his can and tossed it off to the side.

Twenty-two

Kevin and the band were already ensconced in the backstage room, sipping Dr Peppers. The room had a greasy smell to it. McDonald's bags, cheeseburger wrappers, and envelopes still holding French fries were scattered around the floor.

"Hey, Bono, thank god you made it, man. You believe that stuff outside?" the drummer said.

"Crazy," Wink replied.

Kevin sort of looked past me then said, "So, where is she? I thought you guys were bringing a girlfriend with you?"

"We told her to show up at six," Wink said. "But we had no idea any of this would be going on. You guys aren't on for another two and a half hours, and the place is already twice as jammed as last night."

"All thanks to Bono's voice," the drummer said and nodded at Wink. Everyone laughed.

"Yeah, about the girl, if she does make it in here, her name is Caroline, but we call her Sassy. She thinks he's the real deal, so play along. Tonight he's Bono all night long. Okay?" I said.

"Hoping to get lucky, are we?"

"In a manner of speaking," Wink said.

"I think we're going to play it a little different tonight," Kevin said. "Rather than wait an hour or so. I'm thinking you should come out about fifteen minutes into our first set. Dev, maybe ten minutes before we go on, it would be good if you went out there and pretended to do a security check. You know, look around and stuff. Probably be best to stay on the stage, no telling how crazy people are going to get. You bring that earplug with you?"

"Got it right here," I said, tapping the side pocket in my suit coat.

We waited for another hour and forty-five minutes. By the time I stepped onto the stage wearing sunglasses, the crowd had been chanting "Bono. Bono. Bono." For a good ten minutes.

Different from the night before where no one seemed to be that interested until Wink showed up, tonight the place was packed, and everyone was crowding the stage. If there were three hundred people last night, this crowd looked to easily double that. I was sure Psycho Shelia's had a number of fire code violations going on tonight. Not just the area in front of the stage, but literally, the entire room was packed all the way back to the bar. Suddenly, I caught the signs of some sort of disruption off to the right.

People seemed to be getting pushed left or right from some sort of force. As the disruption moved closer to the stage, I could make out four heads. The one in the middle seemed to be strolling towards me, effortlessly, as his large, muscle-bound compatriots, shoved people out of the way. As they drew closer, they pushed two guys who, for just a brief moment, looked like they might raise an objection. That thought seemed to evaporate into thin air as the two evaluated the odds and decided being on the losing end of things wouldn't be the best way to start the evening.

The guy in the middle of the thugs looked familiar. Short black hair, literally no neck, arms easily the size of my thighs and a hook nose that had been rearranged more than once, and then there was that fat head suddenly looking up and smiling at me.

Fat Freddy Zimmerman. Full time enforcer for local crime lord, Tubby Gustafson. "Haskell, you piece of shit, saw you on the tv today. Had to ask myself, why wouldn't you share the good news with us? And here all this time I thought we were friends."

"Nice to see you, too, Freddy."

"Appreciate you offering to do a favor for us."

"A favor? What are you talking about?" I said and leaned forward just as the crowd started to cheer and scream, drowning out whatever Fat Freddy's answer was. I could see his lips moving, but I couldn't hear a word he said. I turned to look over my shoulder just as the band came onto the stage. Wink was nowhere to be seen and the chant of "Bono. Bono. Bono." immediately filled the room. I could actually feel the vibration from the one-word chorus.

I pointed to my ear and shook my head, hoping Fat Freddy got the message. One of the thugs reached up and grabbed the lapel on my suit coat. I knocked his hand off, stood up, and stepped back.

Freddy got a very mean look on his face and shook his head. I read his lips, something about a mother . . . As large as the thugs were, the crowd still managed to push Freddy and his muscle-bound crew a few feet off to the side. Fat Freddy motioned the thugs to clear a path for him, and they barreled their way through the crowd toward the back of the room.

Twenty-three

The band played two tunes, over the course of the next fifteen minutes before Kevin signaled me to bring Wink onto the stage. During that time, not only did the Bono chant continue, nonstop, but it grew in intensity. We were all beginning to worry we might have an incident on our hands if Wink didn't appear and soon.

I hurried offstage and called his name a half dozen times as I made my way into the break room. Not that I could be heard with the crowd chanting, "Bono. Bono." Once I entered the room, it became clear he was otherwise detained.

Her back was to me as I entered the room, not that it mattered. Sassy was in a pair of booty denim mini short shorts, not much bigger than her thong, if she was even wearing one. Her top was a loose fitting floral something, theoretically knotted between her breasts, only the knot had been untied. She appeared to be rubbing her body up and down against Wink, who she had pinned against the far wall.

"Wink. Hey, Wink. You listening? Come on, man. They need you out on the stage before a riot starts. It's getting crazy out there," I shouted. Neither one of them reacted, but then again with the crowd screaming, they probably couldn't hear me.

I tapped Sassy on the shoulder. Thinking it was Wink, she reached up with both hands and pulled her loose top off and dropped it on the floor. She began to rub her body from left to right against Wink, pinning him even tighter against the wall.

"Hey, hey, guys, come on up for some air, knock it off," I said, pulling Sassy back from Wink.

She immediately glared at me, looked about to say something, then stopped.

"Wink, err, Bono," I shouted. "They need you out on the stage. Now."

Wink was wide-eyed, flushed, and his face was covered with red lipstick blotches. He seemed to take a deep breath, tucked in his t-shirt, and buckled his belt.

I ignored Sassy, took him firmly by the arm, and pulled him towards the short set of stairs leading back onto the stage. "Come on, man, it's getting crazy out there. We need you to calm things down."

We hurried away from Sassy, standing with a shocked look on her face and completely unaware her top was still on the floor.

We hurried up the three steps and onto the stage. A thunderous roar from the crowd occurred as Wink came into view. He raised his hands in a victory salute as the band members seemed to focus in on the red lipstick splotches scattered across his face. He stepped to the front of the stage, reached down to give everyone a high five and moved all the way across the stage, slapping hands as he went. He moved back, repeating the process in the opposite direction. When he reached the corner of the stage, he gave Kevin a nod.

Kevin struck a chord on his guitar, gave a look around to get the band's attention, and they began to play the next set. Wink worked the front of the stage a bit longer and made it to Kevin's side just in time to lean in and mouth the words to the chorus. A thong sailed up onto the stage from over on the right somewhere.

I was checking the crowd for Fat Freddy Zimmerman and company. I couldn't see them, but I knew that didn't make a bit of difference. He was still here, somewhere, just waiting for the right moment to make the night a complete and utter disaster.

It didn't seem like we were out there that long, but suddenly it was break time, and after yet another roar from the crowd, we hurried back into the break room. I made a point of being the last person in the room, then locked the door behind me before I loosened my tie and attempted to relax.

"Absolutely crazy," one of the band members said.

"Unbelievable," Kevin said and shook his head.

At first, I thought they were referring to the crowd, but then I followed their eyes and settled on Wink, or at least what I could see of him. His back was toward me. Sassy appeared to be surgically attached with both arms and legs wrapped around him, gyrating in a very rhythmic manner. The band was suddenly quiet and just stared at the two of them.

I grabbed an ice-water from the cooler and placed the chilled plastic bottle against the back of Wink's head. "Hey, Bono, better come up for air and catch a breath. While you're at it, maybe have some of this water. You're not even halfway finished if you count the couple of encores you're gonna have to do."

Over the next two hours, other than losing my hearing during the second half of the concert and the two follow-up encores, things went off without a hitch. We were all seated in the backstage room at this point. Sassy was sitting on Wink's lap, still gyrating. Everyone was so exhausted no one seemed to care, including Wink. The crowd was still cheering "Bono, Bono, Bono," out at the front of the stage, but we could detect the chant beginning to gradually weaken.

Two beers later, the chant had disappeared, and we could hear cars exiting the parking lot. By the third beer, the band was packing up their instruments and hauling cords and microphones off the stage. Maybe a half dozen people were left in the concert area, none of whom paid any attention to the band.

It was after two in the morning, and I was ready to go home. Sassy looked to be asleep on Wink's lap, although she still had a tight hold on him.

"Hey, Bono. It's probably safe enough to get you out of here. What do you say?"

Wink's eyes fluttered open at the same time Sassy raised her head from his lap and yawned. "Oh, do you have to go?"

Wink gave a halfhearted nod.

"Maybe you could say your goodbye, Bono, and I'll meet you out in the parking lot. Just remember once you open that door, you should hurry into my car before some crazy fans jump you. I'll see you in a couple of minutes. I'll give you a call tomorrow, Sassy."

She sort of shrugged as if to say, 'whatever'. I said my goodbye to Kevin and the band, then headed out to my car.

The moment I came out of Psycho Shelia's two very large men, one on either side of me stepped up and said, "Mr. Zimmerman would like a word with you."

I recognized the two thugs as part of Fat Freddy's crew. They'd been pushing people aside and clearing the path for Fat Freddy just before the band came on.

"Hey, look, guys, can't this wait? It's been a really long day. I'm dragging ass and I—"

One of them slapped me on the back of my head, hard, almost knocking me over.

"Ouch. Hey, what the hell did you do that for?"

My question just encouraged the other thug to repeat the process, even harder.

"Hey, knock it off, don't do that," I said just as a black Escalade pulled alongside.

The thug who slapped me first pulled the sliding door on the passenger side open and said, "Get your dumb ass in there."

"And if I don't?"

A fist suddenly slammed into my solar plexus. I groaned for a nanosecond before I was desperate for air. The second thug half pushed, half tossed me into the back seat and onto the floor.

"Get your ass in here, dumb shit." The driver shouted as if I'd somehow been holding up the process.

Twenty-four

Delton put the key in the ignition as he said, "It's about damn time. Okay, there's Haskell. Come on, let's go." He turned the key in the ignition. "Come on, damn it, start," he said as the engine groaned. He turned the key three more times before a cloud of exhaust exploded behind them, and the Olds 88 gradually came to life.

"Hold up, dude. Who the hell is that, more security?" Clarence said and took another sip of his beer.

They watched as the black Escalade screeched to a stop, and two very large men jumped out. First one and then the other slapped Haskell on the back of his head, then forced him into the back of the Escalade and sped out of the near-empty parking lot.

"Whoever it was, they didn't look too happy. They just made our job that much easier. Bono will probably be out in just a minute," Delton said. He put the car in park and waited.

A few minutes later, the delivery door opened, and Bono stepped out with a drop-dead gorgeous blonde attached to him. They stood next to Haskell's Jeep, looked around for a brief second or two then hurried toward a back corner in the lot.

"I don't believe it, is this a good omen or what? They're coming right to us," Delton said.

"You think they're going where I think they're going?"

"That blue sports car with the white top. It's the only other car back here. This is just perfect. Must be the rich bitch's set of wheels. Just sit tight."

Wink and Sassy walked toward her Mercedes with their arms around one another. Wink, still playing the role, said, "I'm sure he was going to give me a ride. I don't understand, I've got an early morning flight scheduled."

"He wanted to do that, baby, but I think he just sent me a text, I felt the vibration," Sassy said and raised an eyebrow. "He said I should give you a ride to my place, and he'd join us just as soon as he can. It's nice and private. We can get to know one another better in my jacuzzi, drink some wine, get you relaxed after working so hard. We can maybe think of a couple other things you'd like to do."

"Sounds like a plan. Come on, let's go. A hot bath and a full body rub might be just the thing. Who knows where it will go from there?" Wink said and picked up the pace just as a big old rusted bomb pulled up alongside.

"Hey, hold up. I mean, excuse me," Clarence said as he stepped out of the passenger side. "We're security here at Psycho Shelia's. Supposed to make sure you get to your car safely."

"I'm parked right over there, the Mercedes with the white top," Sassy said.

Clarence set his beer can on the hood of the Olds 88. "We still gotta give you a lift, it's the rules."

"It's twenty feet away?"

"You just better get in," he said and began to pull the rear door open. The door gave a loud groan as he opened it, and Sassy began to shake her head no.

"Hey, I ain't telling you again, bitch."

"What the hell do you think you're doing? Do you have any idea who I am? I'm gonna report your ass to the crabby bastard that runs this place. You can't talk to my friend like that," Wink said.

"Girlfriend," Sassy corrected and wrapped her arm tighter around Wink's waist.

Clarence stepped forward and wrapped his massive arms around both of them, picked them up, dumped first Sassy and then Wink into the back seat and slammed the door closed. He hurried around to the passenger side and climbed in. Delton accelerated out of the parking lot before Clarence had the door completely closed.

"What the hell do you think you're doing?" Wink shouted. He searched the inside of the door only to discover the door handle had been removed.

"Oh, you think this is funny? You two are in so much trouble," Sassy shouted. "I'm calling the police," she said and pulled out her cellphone.

"Get that," Delton shouted. Clarence reached back and grabbed the cell from Sassy before she could punch in 911. "Hey, Mr. Bono, better hand over your phone, too."

"Guys, you're making a huge mistake. You don't know what you've gotten yourself into here. Just pull over and let us out," he said as they sped down the entrance ramp and onto the Interstate.

"Give me your damn cellphone," Clarence said and held out a massive calloused paw.

"Look, I'm telling you, you're making a big mistake. Now just let us out and we'll—"

Clarence grabbed a fistful of Sassy's hair and squeezed it tight.

"Ouch, ouch, ouch. Stop it, you animal. Stop it. I just had it done," Sassy cried.

"Then tell dumb shit to give me his cellphone."

"Do it, Bono, do it, baby. My stylist cost me two hundred dollars this afternoon. Ouch, will you stop pulling my hair, you animal."

"Give me the damn cellphone," Clarence shouted.

"Okay, okay, here, you can have it," Wink said and handed his cell to Clarence.

If Sassy was surprised he used a cheap android phone with a cracked screen she didn't let on.

Clarence took both phones, tossed them in the front seat then shoved two sweat-stained pillowcases into the back seat. "Put them things over your head so you can't see where the hell we're going."

Sassy grimaced and lifted the pillowcase from her lap using just her thumb and forefinger. She dropped it on the seat between her and Wink and gave a slight shudder. "You've got to be kidding. Over my head? Really? Look at the stains on it. I've no idea where this has been, and based on the smell, I'm pretty sure it's never been washed. I'm not putting this over my head. I just had a Grand Luxe facial this afternoon. I can assure you I will not be . . ."

"Lady," Delton said, glancing at her in the rearview mirror. "You are very quickly becoming a major pain in the ass. Now, either you start cooperating, and damn fast, or you're going to need some major surgery on that nose of yours."

"How dare you say—"

"Sassy, I think we better do what they say," Wink said and picked up the pillowcase on his lap.

"If you think I'm—"

Clarence reached over, took hold of another fistful of hair and pulled. "Ouch, ouch, ouch. Okay, let go. Let go, you animal and I'll do it. Do you ever listen at all? I told you I just had my hair done."

He let go and made a show of tossing the loose strands from his hand into the back seat. Sassy gingerly picked up the pillowcase. "Oh, oh, oh, this is so gross. I'm liable to get sick," she said, trying to make sure that the pillowcase touched as little of her face as possible. She leaned into the corner of the back seat with the pillowcase over her head, and quietly began to sob.

"Good, now both of you just stay calm and not another word," Delton said. He looked over and gave Clarence a thumbs up. For his part, Clarence turned toward the back seat and moved his head from side to side, attempting to find the best angle to examine Sassy's loosely knotted top.

Twenty-five

I was on my back, gasping for air as the door slammed closed, and the Escalade accelerated out of Psycho Shelia's parking lot. A large pair of shoes suddenly landed on my stomach and proceeded to wipe themselves back and forth across my suit coat, shirt, and Christmas tie.

"It just can never be easy with you, can it, Haskell?"

I glanced up from the floor and attempted to focus on Fat Freddy Zimmerman. Hard to believe, but it looked like he'd put on more weight. "You enjoy the concert, Mr. Zimmerman?"

"I may have if only you'd taken the time to act a little more civil towards a friend," he said, indicating himself.

"Civil? Come on Fred—, err, Mr. Zimmerman. You were there, everyone started screaming and cheering, and it was impossible to hear myself even think let alone attempt to hear whatever you were trying to say. Besides, I had to run and get Bono ready to head onstage."

"Yeah, Bono. You friends with him?"

"Friends? Well, no, not really. I mean, I'm doing the bodyguard gig, but that pretty much ends tonight. Tomorrow he'll be off to do another concert or record a new song somewhere. I just handle his St. Paul security, they don't tell me anything about his future plans. He's very hush, hush about what's happening next."

"Well, I've got a future plan for him now. Next Tuesday night, Mr. Gustafson—"

"I just got done telling you that — Oufff!" I said that last bit as Fat Freddy stomped on my stomach, hard. Very hard.

"Mistake number one, you interrupted me," Freddy said and stomped on my stomach again. "Mistake number two, you raised your voice," he said and stomped on my stomach yet again. "Mistake number three, you interrupted me," he said and stomped my stomach once more.

"You already said that sir, and I get the point."

He raised both feet like he was going to stomp on me again. I groaned, "No, please, please, don't. I apologize. I'm sorry, sorry, sorry."

"Hmmm, better," he said and waited a long moment. "Good, now that we have the rules down, meaning I talk, and you don't say shit. Hopefully, I'll be able to proceed, uninterrupted."

"You, I suppose, but more importantly, your close personal friend, Bono, are invited to Cynthia Gustafson's fifteenth birthday party this coming Tuesday evening."

"What?"

"Why do you insist on being so stupid. You heard me, Haskell. Mr. Gustafson's granddaughter, Cynthia, is turning fifteen and Bono's appearance to wish her happy birthday, a very happy birthday will be just the thing to make the night memorable."

"I don't think he'll be in town. I think he has a gig in Vegas, or Nashville, or was it L.A?"

Fat Freddy shook his head. "Apparently, we're not listening, Haskell. Tuesday night, Cynthia Gustafson is turning fifteen. You will have Mr. Bono there to make the evening memorable for the young lady. You can expect a small crowd of perhaps just a hundred and fifty or so. It'll be a private event, held at the Reform School."

"That bar on East Seventh?"

"Exactly."

We drove in silence for a few more minutes until Fat Freddy said, "Okay, this is good enough." The Escalade suddenly swerved to the right and skidded to a stop.

"If you would, please, get out, Haskell. I think we've all had just about enough of you." Freddy groaned as he turned to the right, removing his shoes from my suit coat. The side door slid open, and the thug who'd punched me in the solar plexus hopped out, grabbed me by the ankles and started to pull me out of the Escalade. I kicked my legs until he let go, then hurried out of the vehicle and looked around.

"Where in the hell are we?" I said. I was standing in the middle of a very large parking lot for some shopping mall. Other than the Escalade, there wasn't another car in sight.

"Just head west, you'll get there, eventually," Fat Freddy said and laughed. The thug hopped back in and pulled the door closed as they took off.

I stood there, watching the taillights head up the road until they disappeared. I pulled out my phone, called Wink, but ended up leaving a message. "Hey, Bono, I got kidnapped by some thugs. Give me a call as soon as you get this." It was almost three-thirty in the morning. I glanced around the empty parking lot then headed up the road in the same direction as Fat Freddy's Escalade.

Twenty-six

I walked a good mile before I made it to the Interstate, then took a left and headed west along the frontage road for another four or five miles. It was damn near 5:30 in the morning before I wandered into the parking lot behind Psycho Shelia's. The sky was clear, the sun was just above the horizon, and my car was right where I had left it. But then, with a flat tire, how could it have been moved, unless it was towed away? There was just one other car in the lot, and it was parked back in the far corner. A dark blue Mercedes S 65 AMG coupe with a white convertible top. It had to be Sassy's. So, where was she? Or, more importantly, where was Wink?

I walked back to her car, hoping maybe the two of them might still be wrapped up in some coital embrace in the front seat. But as I approached, I noticed the windows weren't steamed up, and a quick glance inside confirmed my fear. Empty.

I walked back to the Jeep, spent the next forty minutes changing the flat tire, and drove home. I pulled into my driveway, groaned my way up the front porch steps and unlocked the door. Morton was asleep just on the other side of the door, and as I opened the door, it began to slide him across the floor and woke him up. He stepped just far enough to be out of the way, then stretched and shook himself all the while giving me a look that suggested I was a first-class jerk.

I was too tired to argue the point, and anyway, I was thinking he just might be right.

"Come on, boy, outside," I said and headed for the kitchen. After a moment, he followed me into the kitchen and wandered out to the back yard. I made coffee, set the timer to begin perking at ten then let Morton back in.

I filled his food and water dish. He shot me a look that suggested something like, 'This is it? Really?' But I was too tired to care and went upstairs to bed.

The alarm on my cell woke me later that morning. I felt like I could have slept for another eight hours as I sat on the edge of the bed. I was still dressed in my suit. Only now, it had footprints from Fat Freddy's shoes and was grease-stained from changing the tire. Somewhere along the way, I'd torn a knee in the trousers. I phoned Wink and Sassy again, but neither one bothered to answer. I figured Wink remained in character and played the part of Bono beautifully, enjoying Sassy's late-night festivities that were supposed to have been reserved for me.

I stumbled into the bathroom, took a long hot shower, pulled on a pair of shorts and a t-shirt, and wandered back downstairs. I phoned Wink and Sassy, again, but got dumped into their voice messaging after two rings. They must have really had a night.

I thought about going down to the office, then remembered it was Sunday. My phone rang that afternoon. I'd been asleep on the couch. I hoped it was Wink.

"Haskell Investigations."

"We checked, Haskell. Your pal, Bono, hasn't been at the airport yet. I hope you had the opportunity to talk some sense into him, so he'll be in town Tuesday."

"Fred . . . Mr. Zimmerman?"

"How perceptive."

"Yeah, I had a chat with him, and he's in the process of trying to adjust his schedule. I think he can make it, maybe. By the way, you didn't, by any chance, let the air out of my tire last night, did you?"

"What?"

"Well, when I finally got back to my car the tire was flat and I . . ."

"And now that's my fault? No, I didn't do that. If I had, all four tires would have been flat."

"It was just the one, sir."

"So, there you go, proof positive it wasn't me. We're all counting on you to deliver your guest to the birthday party Tuesday night. I sincerely hope I don't have to remind you of the importance of a little girl's fifteenth birthday. Without going into any detail, it would be an awful shame if you didn't come through. Mr. Gustafson is counting on you," Fat Freddy said and hung up.

Great. Just who I wanted to hear from. Not. I stumbled into the kitchen for a late lunch. About all I had in the refrigerator was a couple of hot dogs and some coleslaw that was about a week old. The coleslaw smelled okay, maybe. I boiled the hot dogs, and ate everything in under four minutes, just as I finished, my phone rang.

Twenty-seven

I have a specific ringtone that identifies unknown callers. When I hear that ringtone, I never, ever answer the call. Ever. If the person really wants to get in touch with me, they'll leave a message. The ringtone blasts out a guy singing a song,

"Unknown caller. Why do you bother? I ain't never, never, never, never ever gonna answer you. Unknown caller. Why do you bother? I ain't never, never, never, never ever gonna answer you. Unknown caller. Why do you bother? I ain't never, never, never, ..."

The ringtone supposedly repeats for thirty seconds, although I can't recall an instance where it actually played for that long before I disconnected. For the first and only time I can recall, I answered. Maybe I was half asleep. Maybe I hoped it was Sassy calling to invite me over and make up to me for her error in judgment last night. Whatever the reason, I answered the phone.

"Haskell Investigations."

"Dev, yeah, it's Bono, Dude."

"Hey, Wink, been trying to reach you. You survive all the up close and personal attention from Sassy last night?"

"Dev, there's been—"

"I gotta tell you, man, the way the two of you were going at it—"

"Ahem, there seems to have been a bit of an incident, Mr. Haskell, and if you'd just give me a—"

"Bit of an incident? From the looks of it, you're lucky to even be alive. I'm amazed you—"

"Jesus Christ, Dev. Will you just shut the hell up for a minute and listen?"

"Whoa. Relax, man. I'm cool about last night if that's what you're worried about. I just want to hear all the sexy details."

"Dev, will you, please, shut the hell up? I'm trying to tell you, we've got a problem and—"

A different voice suddenly came on the line. "Lock him back in the bedroom. You Hassle? Bono's security guy? Nice job, by the way. You made it awfully easy. Whatever he paid you, you should probably give it all back."

"Who the hell is this?"

"None of your damn business."

"Put him back on." I said. "Just what in the hell do you—"

"Shut up and listen, dumb shit. For the next few hours or days, we're the most important thing in Bono's life. So get your fat head out of your dumb ass and pay attention. Thanks to you screwing up, we got your pal, Bono. We'll contact you later with a way to get him back. Do not contact the cops. You do that, and you can kiss him goodbye, and his hot chick, too. Your job right now is to come up with a million bucks, cash, Hassle. You hear me? Cash." Click.

"Hello? Hey, Wink? Wink? Come on, man, quit screwing around. Hello? Wink?"

Twenty-eight

Clarence asked, "So what'd he say? We gonna get the dough?"

"You were standing right next to me, did you, at any time, hear him tell me we were gonna get the dough? Well, did you?"

"Mmm-mmm, come to think of it, he sort of maybe forgot that part."

"Not really. Look, we gotta let 'em know Bono and Miss Pain in the Ass are with us. Once they realize that, things'll start to fall into place."

"Did he offer to pay?"

"He didn't have a chance. I just want him to know we got Bono. That's all. It's probably gonna take 'em a day or two to get the dough lined up. So, we just gotta be patient."

"Hey, you out there," Sassy suddenly called from behind the locked door. "I need to use the bathroom."

"Oh, man," Clarence groaned. "I tell you that broad. How in the hell does Bono even put up with her?"

"Dude's rich enough. He's got servants who probably have to deal with her. Poor bastard should pay us to take her off his hands. There you go, all the money in the world, and he ends up with that," Delton said.

"Did you hear me? I need to use the bathroom, now," Sassy called with a little more urgency.

"Better bring her in there before she wets the bed."

"Why do I always have to do it?"

"Because Clarence, while you're escorting her to and from the bathroom, I'm planning our next move."

"Our next move?"

"Yeah, you know, the ransom note. Now, get her into the bathroom. When she's finished, lock her back up in the bed and come out here. We gotta write a note."

"Who you sending a note to?"

"The ransom note, Clarence. You know, so they can pay us."

"You're gonna mail it?"

Delton closed his eyes for a moment, took a deep breath, and said, "Just, just get her into the bathroom and then lock her back up. Okay?"

"Not a problem, man."

"Hello. Is anybody even out there? I have to pee, really, really bad."

Sassy had a chain wrapped around her waist and shoulders that was padlocked to a bolt in the floor. Wink was secured the same way. The chain had enough slack to allow them to lay down on the double bed or stand up and take two or three steps away from the bed. Theoretically, there was a window in the small room they occupied, but that was merely an assumption on their part based on the 4x8 sheet of plywood screwed into the wall of the log cabin.

For the moment, Sassy was standing with her legs tightly crossed and gritting her teeth. She figured she could maybe hold things for another minute, possibly two, but then she was out of time. She glanced over at Bono, apparently asleep on the bed. Thankfully the door opened.

"God, it's about damn time, hurry up, I really have to go," she said.

Clarence gave her a look that was less than enduring, then crouched down to unlock the chain.

"Come on, come on, come on," she whined while Clarence fumbled for a moment with the padlock. Once he opened the lock, she hurried out the door toward the small bathroom, dragging the chain behind her.

"No funny business in there," Clarence said as she quickly closed the bathroom door.

"Oh, thank God," she said to herself as she hurried towards the pink porcelain toilet, circa 1960. The toilet and small sink were the same dreadful pink, no doubt unattractive since the day they'd been installed. The metal shower stall appeared to have been white at one time, although that had gradually changed to rust over the years. Some sort of green mold seemed to be growing in all four corners of the shower.

When she was finished, she stood in front of the cracked mirror and shuddered at her appearance. She'd had a facial and her highlights done less than twenty-four hours ago, not that you could tell. Riding in the back seat of that dreadful vehicle for hours with a soiled pillowcase over her head had left its mark, and she felt physically ill for a moment as she recalled the incident. She'd been given cold cereal for breakfast. Peanut butter flavored Cheerios to be exact, all chased down with dreadful, flavorless coffee in a cracked cup. God!

There was a sudden knock on the bathroom door, followed by, "Hey, you just about done in there?"

She gently rubbed her hand along her cheek, last night's makeup, good lord, unbelievable. No cleansing, no creams, not so much as a toothbrush. She took the last of the toilet paper and covered her hand then, cautiously turned the grimy doorknob and opened the door.

"You're out of toilet paper," she said and handed the wad of paper and the empty tube to Clarence. He led her back into the bedroom, reattached her chain to the floor then locked the bedroom door behind him.

"What do think we should do, Bono, honey?" she whispered as she rolled over on the bed to face Wink.

Wink opened one eye and figured there just might be an opportunity.

Twenty-nine

Leave it to Wink to steal my night with Sassy and then joke about it. I thought about the phone call for a brief moment then drifted back to sleep. Morton barking and jumping on the couch woke me sometime later. The sun was setting, and I could hear the hum of dinner conversation coming from the restaurant patio across the street. I must have been out for a couple of hours.

"Morton, give it a rest. Come on, outside, let's go outside." At the mention of outside, he immediately jumped off me and ran over to the front door. "No, come on, out back, let's go out back," I said and headed for the kitchen. Morton continued to bark at the front door. "What is with you, Morton? Come on, this way."

He continued to bark, and when I finally glanced out the front door, I saw a small box on the porch. A Sunday delivery? Yeah, maybe, although I hadn't ordered anything. I stepped onto the porch and picked up the box. It didn't even weigh a pound. There was no address label, just my last name written in black magic marker. By the looks of the penmanship, some kid had written it, and I noticed my name was misspelled. I shook the box, but nothing rattled.

I tore off the blue masking tape and opened the box as I stepped back in the house. I pulled out the garment, and took a long look. A black vest with silver buttons. Wink's Bono costume. A piece of paper fluttered to the floor. More black magic marker, I could read the primitive writing from where I stood.

We got bono

get 1 millon in 20 doller bills

wil call with derectens

dont call cops.

I thought back to the phone call, maybe it was for real. Wink was capable of pulling a practical joke, but he wouldn't have sent me the note and enclosed his vest. Based on the spelling and the primitive penmanship, it looked like we weren't dealing with the brightest bulb on the tree. I debated calling Aaron LaZelle, my pal on the police force, then quickly decided against it.

I pulled my phone out, went to recent calls, and clicked on one of the calls. "What?" Was how the crabby voice answered after a few rings. He didn't sound too happy.

"Hi, Mr. Zimmerman. Hey, I just had a package delivered. I think we might have a problem."

"A package? And just why in the hell would that be my problem?" Fat Freddy said.

"It's just that I think someone kidnapped Bono, and I don't think he's going to be able to make it to the birthday party on Tuesday."

"Kidnapped? Who the hell did that?"

"If I knew that I wouldn't be calling you. I'd be out there getting Bono back."

"You better get this damn problem solved and fast, Haskell. Correct me if I'm wrong, but weren't you supposed to be providing security for him? What the hell were you doing?"

"What was I doing? I was on the floor of your fancy Cadillac Escalade with your feet on top of me, and then, when you finally decided to let me out, I had to walk a half dozen miles back to Psycho Shelia's to get my car. You and those two idiots who thought it was funny to slap me around left Bono completely unprotected for four or five hours and, well, now, this is the end result."

"So, what do you expect me to do about it?"

"What do I expect? Oh, nothing, really. I just thought I'd be a nice guy and give you a heads up because the next call I'm gonna have to make is to Tubby. I'll have to tell him his great idea for his granddaughter meeting Bono on her fifteenth birthday has been absolutely, completely screwed up by you and your two pals."

"Now, just hold on a damn minute. You don't have to—"

"Actually, I do, Freddy. I mean it's the polite thing to do, give him a chance to come up with another idea for a birthday gift. You know, instead of meeting Bono he could maybe get her a nice Bono t-shirt or something. I'm sure he'll understand."

There was a long silence.

"Well, I guess I better make that call. You have a good rest of the day, Freddy."

"Wait a minute, Haskell. Can you just wait a damn minute? I'm thinking here."

I wanted to say, 'Does it hurt?' But thought better of that particular move.

"Where are you now?" Fat Freddy said.

"I'm at my place?"

"That dive you live in, or that trash heap you call an office."

"My house. I'm looking at the vest he wore last night and a ransom note."

"A ransom note? Oh, for Christ's sake. All right, let me see what I can find out. In the meantime, you are to stay put. Understand? I don't want you going off like you usually do, making a bad situation even worse. Stay there, don't talk to anyone. Don't phone anyone. I want you to just sit there and think about who in the hell did this. Got it?"

"What are you going to do?"

"Well, apparently, I'm going to have to fix this mess you created."

"I created? Hey, you guys—"

"Haskell, enough. Just do like I said, sit there and shut the hell up. Got it?"

"Yeah, okay. I got it."

Thirty

Sitting at home looking out the window and waiting for Fat Freddy Zimmerman to call me didn't exactly sound like the best idea. I needed to start by trying to find out who grabbed Wink and Sassy. I didn't have a clue how to go about that task, but I knew someone who might. I clicked on his number in my contact list and made the call. After three rings, the theme song from 'Revenge of the Nerds' kicked in for twenty seconds before I could leave a message.

"Yeah, Preston, Dev Haskell. I could really use your help, and I'm on a tight time frame. Please, please, please, give me a call back as soon as possible."

The call came through about five minutes later. Preston Leadbetter.

"Preston, thanks for calling back, man. I got a problem."

"There's a surprise. What's up, dude?" It sounded like a tv was playing in the background.

I gave a quick explanation of recent events, leaving out any interaction with Fat Freddy, Wink pretending to be Bono, and absolutely everything related to Sassy. "So, my pal calls me for help, but before he can tell me anything, this other jerk takes the phone from him and says they'll contact me with a way to get him back. A couple hours later, I find a package on my front porch with a ransom note and the vest he was wearing last night."

"A vest? You kiddin'? That sucks, dude. Even I don't wear vests. Don't they usually just cut off a finger or a toe or something and send that to you."

"Fortunately, things haven't escalated to that stage yet, Preston."

"So what do you want me to do? Hey, hang on for a second." He must have set the phone down because I could hear him half shouting, "There, you like that. You stupid bastard. You are so finished. Okay, Dev, sorry about that. Business. Like I said before, what do you want me to do?"

"I'm wondering if you can track the phone and find out where in the hell they are?"

"Shouldn't you maybe go to the police with this? Seems to me they'd be the best ones to handle this sort of thing."

"Yeah. Unfortunately, they told me not to go to the police, and I'm thinking they just might have an informant there who would let them know if I did," I lied. "So, I'm trying to be careful. Well, and plus, they want a million dollars in ransom money."

"A million bucks? Who is this guy?"

"No one. I mean, he's a pal of mine, but he's not rich or anything. I think they made a mistake, maybe thought he was someone else, you know? I'm just hoping I can get him back somehow. The first step in doing that would be to find out where in the hell they're holding him."

"Call came through on your cell?"

"Yeah."

"I suppose you need this pretty soon."

"No, I need it yesterday. Can you do it?"

"I can try, I'm working on something right now. Let me get to a stopping point. If you could bring your cell over here, that would save me some time."

Save him some time was an understatement. Preston didn't have a driver's license, so he rode a bike around town, not that you'd know it to look at him. Exercise had never been a strong point.

"You still living at your mom's?"

"Yeah, just off Warner road. You remember how to get over here?"

"I can be there in twenty minutes."

"Give me thirty. I should be able to wrap this project up by then," Preston said.

The fifteen-minute drive over to Preston's mom's house was uneventful. She owns a small 1920's, two-story, wood-frame house, painted white. Preston lives in her basement, and she keeps the basement door locked. I parked in front then went around the side of the house to the old coal cellar doors. I pulled one of the doors open, went down six steps, and pounded on the thick wooden door at the basement level.

"Yeah, it's open," Preston called.

I creaked the door open and walked down a dingy, moldy smelling hallway into an even dingier room that had been lined with cheap paneling back in the mid-sixties. The walls were decorated with Superhero posters. All the basement windows had been covered with tin foil. The place smelled like a combination of dirty laundry and a fat guy who hadn't showered in a while.

Preston sat oozing out of a high back chair on wheels parked in front of a semicircular desk with his back toward me. Three large computer screens with some sort of superhero game running on them illuminated the room. Three empty pizza delivery boxes and a number of Red Bull cans littered the far end of the desk next to his bed.

"Be with you in a minute, Dev. I just have to get this last guy down, and I'm up to the grand level. Maybe grab a Red Bull out of the fridge for me and help yourself."

Preston's avocado green refrigerator was about thirty-five years old and positioned next to the washer and dryer. I had to kick a pile of laundry across the floor to open the door. The two shelves held a dozen Coke and Red Bull cans, a pizza delivery box, and an almost empty bag of Snickers candy bars. The contents helped explain the three hundred plus pounds Preston carried around. I popped the top on a Red Bull and set it down next to him.

"Thanks, dude. Die baby die. Watch this, Dev. He's about to be finished off. Woo-hoo-hoo. Sayonara, man. Ha-ha-ha," he said as an explosion suddenly erupted across all three screens, and immediately out of the cartoon rubble, a white surrender flag waved back and forth.

Preston swiveled his chair around, faced me, and grinned. "Oh man, that was great." He glanced at his watch. "Little more than four hours, and I smoked everyone. I'm gonna take this tournament, dude, I can feel it."

"You've been playing that game for the last four hours?"

"Hardly play, dude. It's on to the next level for your boy here, and ultimately the championship." He smiled then proceeded to gulp down half of the Red Bull. I could hear him swallowing, but his triple chin hid any throat movement.

"So, your cell," he said, setting the Red Bull off to the side. "You said you wanted to track the call, see if we can find out where these people are. Let's have a look, dude."

I pulled the cell out of my front pocket and handed it to him. He gave me a funny look then took the phone. "Are you're kidding me? This is the phone you use?"

"Yeah, I get calls and make calls, once in a while I send an occasional text message. I'm never on the internet or Facebook or Twitter on the thing. I just make calls and receive calls."

He gave a loud sigh. "An android. An obsolete android at that. Okay, let's see what we got." He spun around in his chair, plugged a cable into the phone then started clicking the keyboard. Codes and text flashed up on the screen, a mishmash of letters and numbers that made absolutely no sense to me.

"Hmm-mmm, interesting," he said, pausing on Fat Freddy's number for a moment before moving on. "This it here, local number, 651 area code?"

"Yeah, the call couldn't have been more than a minute or so. Came in around two o'clock this afternoon."

"How about two forty-seven?"

"Could of, I suppose, if you say so. Can you see what cell towers it's bouncing off of?"

He gave me a look and said, "I'm into the twenty-first century, dude. A little more current than that old cell tower technology. Let me do some tracking here," he clicked a number of keys, a map appeared, then began flashing back and forth.

"The feds passed some legislation back in I don't know, maybe two thousand one or two. Service providers gotta be able to give a position within three hundred and twenty-eight feet. It gets pretty damn accurate now, provided the phone is on, and the battery isn't dead."

"Three hundred and twenty-eight feet, the cell towers can track that close?"

Another disdainful look. "No, you're talking ancient technology, dude. Now we use GPS. The manufacturers incorporated triangulation capabilities into telephone handsets. Instead of relying on three local phone cells, GPS relies on very precise signals from twelve or more satellites in low earth orbit. Of course, that means with a lot more reference points, the phone can identify its own location to within a few feet. The phone always uses a software application that runs in the background to report its location to the service provider. Because it's GPS, the location is pretty accurate."

"No offense, Preston, but how do you know all this shit?"

"Just staying current, dude, you oughta try it some time."

"I'm lucky I can turn the damn thing on. Like I said, I just make calls and get calls."

He clicked some more keys and said, "Hmm-mmm, numbers not listed with Team Mobile, let's give Verizon a try." He clicked some more keys, a few thousand lines of text appeared on the screen.

"You ever get a headache doing all this?"

"Dude, it's what I love to do. Oh, look at this, here we go. There, that wasn't so bad. You said this number is the kidnapper?"

"Yeah, I mean, my pal was on the phone at first and then some guy who told me they'd be in touch and a couple hours later the box was on my porch. It sounded like he had someone with him, you know? Besides my pal."

"Where the hell is Dead Fish Lake?" Preston said.

"Dead Fish Lake? Interesting, maybe only two hours north. I was out that way a few years back. A guy's wife was engaging in some extracurricular activities. I took a bunch of pictures. Anyway, not the nicest area, not that the name helps."

"Yeah, kind of puts it toward the bottom of the list of places you'd want to go to for a little vacation. Well, anyway, it looks like that's where your call came from. Problem is, that doesn't mean they're out there now. If they had any brains, they wouldn't call from their hiding place. Two hours away, not that far when you're trying to throw folks off your trail."

"If you got a better idea, I'm all ears."

"Let me put it this way. The phone is still there. Course, they could have just tossed it in a ditch."

"It's an unknown number."

"Still doesn't mean they might have used it and then just tossed it."

"Like I said, you got a better idea, I'm all ears."

Preston seemed to think for a moment and shook his head. His fingers clicked across the keyboard. I looked at the map displayed on the screen. "Can you print that off for me?" I said just as the printer sprang to life.

Thirty-one

We chatted for another ten minutes, Preston telling me lies about all the women he was dating. I knew for a fact the only time he left the basement was to go out the coal cellar doors to meet the pizza delivery guy. Still, he'd given me the only potential clue I had to go on. I thanked him, told him to send me a bill, and hurried out the door. I debated calling Fat Freddy and telling him what I'd learned, but in the end, decided it would be more complication than I really needed.

I drove home, packed the car with a sleeping bag, a change of clothes, put Morton in the back seat, and headed north. It was almost midnight by the time we rolled into the town of Dead Fish, Minnesota, population four hundred and seventy-eight.

There was a wide main street that ran about two blocks, with parking on both sides at a forty-five-degree angle to the sidewalk. The street boasted a post office, three bars, a police station with nine to five hours posted on the front door, a couple of empty storefronts, and a Norwegian Lutheran Church.

All the buildings were just one story and looked to be about a hundred and fifty years old. The church was a white frame structure with a bell tower. I pulled to the curb. At close to midnight on a Sunday night, I was the only car on the street, but that probably would have been the case on any night of the week.

I took out the map Preston had printed off for me and got my bearings. The call had been placed from an area about a mile out of town and almost on the lakeshore. With any luck, some sort of cabin.

I headed out of town on the County road. The road curved along the shore, and occasionally, I was able to catch a glimpse of the moon reflecting off the lake through the birch trees. At the one mile point on my odometer, I pulled onto the shoulder. From what I could see, there was no sign of life, anywhere.

I left Morton asleep in the backseat, climbed out, and headed towards the lake. It was a short ten-minute walk, that would have taken half the time in the daylight.

I stood on the shore of the lake and looked left and right. There were a handful of lights coming from the town now almost directly across from where I stood. Unfortunately, nothing that suggested a cabin in my immediate vicinity, and it was just too dark in the woods to prowl around looking. I climbed back in the car, drove through town, and went another seven miles to the Night Rider Inn. The name gave me pause. The sign advertised free color tv and patrons parked in front of their room.

Currently, only two cars were parked in front of the ten rooms.

I stepped inside the small office and hit the bell on the reception counter. The counter had what looked like bulletproof glass and an opening to pass room keys and credit cards back and forth. A moment later, a guy I figured for mid-sixty and in need of a shave stepped behind the counter.

"Need a room?" he said, asking the obvious.

"Yes, please."

"Stayed here before?"

"No, first time."

"Fill this form out," he said and slid a four by five-inch card and a pen toward me. The card wanted basic information, name, and address. I filled it out and slid it back to him.

"I'll need a credit card and two forms of identification."

I slid my driver's license, my insurance card, and my credit card across the counter. He glanced at the license and the insurance card, studied my face and the license for a moment then slid them back.

"How many nights?"

"Just one to start. Might be more than that, but hopefully not."

"I know what you mean," he said, ran my credit card, and slid it back to me along with a key to room number nine. "Enjoy your stay," he said, sounding like he didn't mean a word of it.

I got back in my car, drove about fifty feet, and pulled in front of room number nine. I grabbed my overnight bag and stepped into the room. The walls were covered with cheap wood paneling, reminiscent of Preston's basement, and undoubtedly from the same era. There was a desk, a dresser with a small tv, a double bed, and a heavy, stale smell of cigarette smoke. I left the door to the room open, opened the rear door to the car, and woke Morton.

He groaned and took his time hopping out of the back seat. He stretched for a long moment before he followed me into the room. I locked the door and turned on the tv. Morton jumped up on the bed, circled a few times, and settled in.

I heard a noise outside about forty-five minutes later and pulled the curtain back to watch a couple kissing for a long moment before they got into their separate cars and drove off in opposite directions. My car was now the only one parked at the motel.

I pulled my t-shirt off and settled in next to Morton.

Thirty-two

I woke, or rather Morton woke me a little after six the following morning. I walked him outside for five or ten minutes, then filled his food and water dish and took a shower. Forty-five minutes later, we were back in the car and pulled over on the side of the road approximately where we'd stopped the night before.

I left Morton in the car and headed down to the lakeshore. There was no activity on the lake at this hour, but there was a dead fish on the shore that looked like it had been there for some time. More importantly, off to the left, there was smoke rising up above the trees. I headed in that direction.

Cabin was a generous term. The structure was built of logs, but it looked more like a lean-to kids had put up. The roof was patched with different colored shingles, and the six pane window next to the front door, held a piece of what looked like cardboard covering the lower-left pane. The logs appeared dried out and tired looking.

A rusty old blue car, large enough to land a helicopter on the hood, was parked next to the cabin. As I looked, a fairly large guy, with reddish-blonde hair and a beard, climbed out of the back seat of the car, buckled his jeans, and headed into the small cabin. I carefully moved closer and settled in next to some birch trees and waited, and then waited some more. After two hours and nothing happening, I moved closer to the car, wrote down the license plate number, and walked out to the County road. Morton began barking as I approached. I let him out, played fetch with a tennis ball for ten minutes then got him back in the car.

Thirty-three

Sassy smiled and said, "Please tell me you're kidding. Really? This, this unhealthy, peanut butter flavored nonsense again for breakfast. I can't stand it. You simply have to come up with something else. What? You never heard of a nice egg white omelet with feta cheese and black olives, a little sage maybe? Perhaps, a breakfast sausage or two, or maybe maple-cured bacon. How about some imported French marmalade?"

Clarence looked at his brother, Delton, shook his head, gritted his teeth, and walked back out to the car.

"What's his problem? I'm telling you, you've got to step up your game here. How about a full Irish breakfast for the two of us? You'd like that, Bono. Wouldn't you?"

"Do you ever shut up?" Delton asked. "You're really hard work."

"I'm hard work? You've got to be kidding? Have you even bothered to take a look around this dreadful structure? Do the words soap and clean have any connotation? My God, we'll be lucky if we don't contract some sort of dreadful virus? And as if this, this poison you're attempting to feed us isn't bad enough, you don't even have WiFi. How in God's name do you expect me to survive without internet access? Now, I'm putting my foot down and demand that you—"

"Put a sock in it, honey. Bono, I gotta tell you, all the money you make, man, you could sure do a lot better than this, you're a hell of a lot more patient than I am. Tell you what, lady, just eat up what's served, like a good little girl, and I'll be back in a minute," Delton said and hurried out the door shaking his head.

"God, I can't believe those two fools. We should lock the door right now," Sassy said.

"I don't know. Maybe you should give it a rest. Not to point out the obvious, but they've got us chained at this table," Wink said. He was almost as tired as the kidnappers when it came to Sassy's nonstop complaining.

"So, Bono, I noticed you ate all your breakfast," Sassy said, changing the subject. "You work up an appetite last night?"

"Yeah, thank you for that," Wink said. Sassy's activity last night almost made getting kidnapped by these fools worthwhile.

"My pleasure," Sassy smiled and raised her eyebrow. "Plenty more where that came from. But if I could make a tiny little suggestion or two, you seemed to be in an awful hurry. I never had a chance . . ."

* * *

Delton attempted to open the door on the Olds 88, but Clarence had locked it. "Come on, Clarence, you can't sit in there all day. Open the damn door."

Clarence crossed his arms, looked the other way, and shook his head no.

"Clarence, come on, man, open the damn door. I've got an idea that you're gonna wanna hear."

Clarence eventually reached over and grudgingly pulled the lock up. Delton opened the door. "Look, man, I know she's driving you nuts, hey, don't feel like the Lone Ranger, she's driving me crazy, too. I think she's even getting on Bono's nerves, the poor bastard. The complaints, the whining, the constant bitching. For Christ's sake, I want to tape her damn mouth shut. But we can't, man. She'll just get all pissed off, and that'll get Bono mad, and then things will go downhill from there. Look at it like this, the bitch is hard work, very hard work. She's a royal pain in the ass and damn near impossible, but after a few days of hard work, we can take it easy for the entire rest of our lives. We just gotta put up with it for a little while longer until we get paid."

"A little while longer? Delton, every minute I gotta listen to her, feels like a year. She don't like breakfast, she don't like peanut butter and jelly for lunch, the popcorn is bad for her skin. She ain't gonna eat sensitized fat—"

"Saturated."

"Yeah, fine, who the hell cares? I'm thinking we should take her out to the middle of the lake and see if she can make it back to shore. I'm telling you, Delton, I'm about ready to flip out. You hear the two of 'em going at it last night? God, I had to come out and sleep in the car."

"Well, maybe you shoulda stayed on the couch. That action barely lasted a minute or two. You need to take a deep breath and just calm down, man. Here, tell you what," Delton took his wallet out and handed a twenty-dollar bill to Clarence. "Why don't you go over to that grocery store in Halden and get some eggs and tomatoes, maybe some fruit and something she'd like. Hopefully, that'll shut her the hell up."

"You sure? Or is that just gonna make her bitch about shit all the more? I'm telling you man. She's nuts."

"Yeah, believe me, I couldn't agree more. So, there you go, it always evens out. She's an absolute knock out, and that's exactly what you want to do to her, knock her out."

That brought a smile to Clarence's face, and he took the twenty and stuffed it in his pocket. "Okay, I'll get us something really good. I promise. You gonna be okay here alone with those two?"

"Yeah, maybe come in and help me chain 'em up in the bedroom, at least we can close the door on her, then you can take off. When you get back we'll make our phone call to that Hassle guy, tell him where to drop the money."

"Where you thinking?"

"I ain't exactly sure, yet. Someplace we can watch him, make sure it's good. I'm thinking we'll give him motor mouth first, get her out of our hair. Then, if all the cash is there and no cops, we'll let Bono out of the car at midnight or something. After that, we hightail it down to Florida or Texas. Sit around on the beach sipping cold ones all day with some good looking ladies who know how to keep their damn mouths shut."

"Sounds like a plan, man."

"Good. Now, come on, help me get 'em back in the bedroom."

Thirty-four

Once I got Morton back in the car, I sent a text message to Preston with the license plate number asking him to find out who the vehicle was registered to. I was about to make a U-turn on the County road and head back to the motel when the rusty blue Olds pulled out and headed in the opposite direction. It looked like the guy with the beard was the only one in the car. I followed him at a discreet distance.

It took close to twenty minutes before the guy pulled into the Piggly Wiggly Grocery Store in the town of Halden. I parked a couple of lanes away, waited until he got out of the car, then followed him into the store. It wasn't like he was hard to miss. He was big, with reddish-blonde hair and a thick beard. His hair looked like it hadn't seen a comb for the better part of a month, and then there was his t-shirt. A faded orange thing with black letters across the back that read, MINNESOTA CORRECTIONAL INSTITUTE. If it was meant to be a joke, no one seemed to be buying it. Everyone gave him a wide berth.

He grabbed a red plastic grocery basket and headed up the produce aisle. He tossed in a head of lettuce, a

bunch of tomatoes, some celery, a bottle of salad dressing, two large containers of ice cream, a big jar of black
olives, a dozen eggs, a box of chocolate EX-LAX and
headed to the cashier. As I hurried up behind him, I
pulled a container of shampoo off the shelf just to have
an item to purchase. A woman with a loaf of bread and
some Oreo cookies jumped in line ahead of me. I was
still close enough to hear any conversation and hoped I
could at least learn what his name was.

No such luck. He paid with a twenty and a couple of
tens. Then stood there while the high school girl at the
cash register bagged his groceries. He never made an effort to say so much as 'Hi' or 'Thanks'. Once she finished, he carried his bag out to the car.

Nothing in the groceries he purchased suggested he
was feeding Wink and Sassy. I wondered if maybe Preston's suggestion had been right. The kidnappers might
have called from a car, maybe just stopped alongside that
stretch of road, and when they were finished with the
call, they just tossed the phone out the window and drove
off. But then, the guy had grabbed the phone from Wink
and half-shouted at someone to, "Lock him back in the
bedroom." So, maybe that little run-down place was
where Wink and Sassy were being held. Not that I could
make any rational guess based on the smattering of information I had.

I followed him out of the parking lot. He stopped at
a liquor store on the edge of town, went in for all of five

minutes, came out carrying a twelve-pack of Special Export and proceeded to head out of town. I followed him back to where he turned off the County road and onto barely more than a trail. If he noticed me following a quarter-mile behind, he gave no indication. I continued on to the town of Dead Fish and parked behind the post office. I grabbed a tennis ball from the back seat, brought Morton down to the empty beach, and played fetch with him for a good half-hour until he was more or less worn out.

We drove back to the motel. I filled Morton's food and water dishes in the room then walked over to the office. The place appeared to be deserted again, but I could hear what sounded like a tv game show coming from the other side of the closed door, like before I hit the bell on the counter.

The same guy opened the door and stepped out of the room. "Checking out?"

"No, 'fraid not. Business is going to take a little longer than I expected. It's gonna be at least one more day. You don't need to worry about cleaning the room."

He stared for a moment as if to say, 'We don't clean the rooms.' Eventually, he just nodded and watched me walk out of the office. I shut my eyes for thirty minutes, then changed into some dark clothes. I grabbed a can of mosquito repellent and a hunting knife, my Glock 19, along with two spare clips, and drove back to the County road. I drove past the small trail where the Olds had turned in, went maybe a hundred yards further, and parked on the opposite side of the road.

I crossed the road and made my way into the woods heading toward the rundown cabin. I took my time and moved very cautiously. It was a good half hour before I was able to get settled into a spot where I could keep an eye on the place. Fortunately, the Olds was still parked next to the cabin. I settled in, scanned the place with a small pair of binoculars, and saw absolutely nothing that suggested Wink or Sassy were in there.

Thirty-five

Sassy read the label on the back of the bottle. "Piggly Wiggly French dressing. Really? I can't believe you would even eat that, but then again, yeah, it figures. God. Did you even bother to check the ingredients? One hundred and sixty calories per serving, twenty-four grams of fat. Hardly a healthy dressing, more like a heart attack just waiting to happen. I don't suppose you would happen to have some Extra Virgin Imported Olive Oil and maybe a twelve year aged balsamic?"

The blank looks coming from the Baggott brothers seemed to answer her question.

"Oh, honest to God, why do I even bother?" she said, setting the bottle of French dressing back on the table. "Where are the tomatoes from?"

"Piggly Wiggly," Clarence said and forced a smile, thinking he wasn't going to let her accuse him of stealing.

Sassy shook her head. "Local? Imported? Are they organic? Hydroponic? What sort of—"

"Lady, you're given me another major league headache. Can you for once, just eat whatever in the hell is served? I drove a long way to get this shit. Maybe you might think about getting off your damn high horse. You could start by saying, thanks for a change. You even know that word, thanks?" Clarence said.

"What are you getting so upset for? I simply like to know what it is before I put it in my mouth?"

"I think you probably know what it is, the question for you would be who?" Clarence said.

Delton and Wink started to laugh, but a glare from Sassy suddenly silenced the room. She took a bite of her salad and chewed. Then said, "Please tell me you washed these lettuce leaves?"

"We did, twice," Delton said.

"Yeah, and we even used soap."

Wink pushed his salad bowl away. It had come to the point where it wasn't so much the idea of being kidnapped by these two idiots. Now, truth be told, it was Sassy's constant, nonstop, whining, and complaining that had finally taken his appetite away.

Clarence cleared the dishes and set them in the sink on top of the dishes from earlier meals. He took three coffee mugs from the cabinet, placed them on the orange Formica counter, and filled each with two large scoops of vanilla-caramel ice cream. He handed a mug to Delton, gave another to Wink, and kept one for himself.

"Oh? I see. So now, I'm being punished for expressing my own opinion, is that it? Bad me for simply wanting to eat healthily. Dear God, what was I thinking?

Well, just to let you know, the last time I checked, we were still in a free country."

"Relax," Clarence said and smiled. "I knew you wouldn't like the ice cream, it would either be the wrong brand, made in the wrong place, the wrong flavor, you don't like the container, or it didn't cost enough. Hey, I get it, I guess that's just the way you're wired. Fine by me, not a problem on this end."

Sassy thought about that for a moment. "Well, if I don't tell you, how will you ever know it's wrong?"

"You know what? You're right. So, I figured whatever kind of ice cream I got, it wouldn't be good enough for you. That being the case, you're not getting any, problem solved."

"And you don't find that sort of behavior rude?"

"Not really, because, what I did get for you," Clarence said, ignoring the look he was getting. "Was even better, some real fancy imported chocolate." He reached into the cabinet and pulled out a small plate piled with the unwrapped squares of chocolate-flavored Ex-Lax.

"Whoa, check it out," Delton said.

"These are all for you and are not to be shared," Clarence said, setting the plate down in front of Sassy. She stared for a brief second, before quickly pulling the plate just a little closer to her.

Wink looked at the plate, thought about taking one, and glanced up catching Clarence's eye.

Clarence shook his head vigorously, back and forth. "No, no, no, Bono. That chocolate is off-limits to every-one except her. I got the ice cream for you, want some more?"

Wink took the last spoonful, shoved it in his mouth, then passed his empty mug over to Clarence, who shov-eled another large scoop of ice cream into Wink's mug.

Sassy reached for a chocolate square, in the process pulling the plate just that much closer as she took a bite. Mmm-mmm, she thought, not the best she'd ever had, but not the worst either. A unique sweetness she couldn't remember tasting before. "Mmm-mmm, interesting. Im-ported? French? Swiss?"

"Yeah."

"Yeah? Which one, French or Swiss?"

"I think both."

"Hmm-mmm, maybe Teuscher, they're out of Zur-ich. Famous for their champagne truffles although this certainly isn't . . ." she placed the remainder of the piece into her mouth and took another from the plate.

"I've been there, Teuscher," she said and smiled, re-membering. "Unique taste to this. I can't quite place it, but I think I've had it before, it'll come back to me in a minute."

"I'm really glad you like it."

"Yeah, interesting. Unique, very unique."

"I got it just for you."

"Yes, well, thank you. Now, if we could just get in sync with the meals. If there was a purveyor of fine foods nearby, perhaps I could write a grocery list for you. By the way, and no offense, but your kitchen area could do with a good bit of cleaning and scrubbing."

"I'm ready to go back to the bedroom," Wink said. He pushed the empty mug across the table toward Clarence, stood, waited to be unlocked, and led back into the bedroom before Sassy returned to her complaining mode.

"Can I take these back with me?" Sassy said.

"Probably not a good idea, but sit here as long as you want and eat them all," Clarence said as he unlocked Wink's chain. "I'll just walk Mr. Bono back to the bedroom."

"I really have had more than enough," Sassy said as she reached for another piece on the plate. This time she placed the entire square in her mouth and made no effort to rise from the table.

Clarence walked Wink back to the bedroom. As Wink stretched out on the bed, Clarence padlocked his chain to the bolt on the floor. He leaned in close to Wink and whispered, "Don't eat any of that chocolate."

"Hey, I heard you the first and second time."

"I mean it, man. It ain't good for you."

"What, now you're taking a lesson from her book and gonna lecture me on sugar content or sweets?"

"I'm just telling you, man, don't."

There was something in the way he said it that got Winks attention. Had they drugged it? Maybe they were gonna do something to Sassy. God only knows she'd been bitching every waking moment since they left Psycho Shelia's. Not that he hadn't enjoyed the sex-filled minute and a half last night, but if he never had to listen to her bitching again, it would be okay with him.

Thirty-six

There were just three pieces left on the plate when Sassy felt the first unpleasant twinge. She could see the kidnappers through the broken, six paned window next to the front door. They looked like they were just having a casual conversation. She swallowed the chocolate in her mouth and pushed the plate away. Maybe that was it, too much rich chocolate. She wondered if maybe she should join Bono in the bedroom and lay down, but then there was another twinge in her lower region. This one just a little stronger, and she thought it might be best to just stay put for a minute or two.

"We leave Bono here," Delton said. "He's chained to the bed. So, it's not like he can go anywhere. We take her down to the city. You know that bridge we take over to the Westside?"

"To get to that bar?"

"Yeah, the Mad Hatter. We put her on a boat. We tell him to be waiting on the bridge, so he can drop the money down to us from up above. He'll be expecting us to pull up in a car, so a boat is gonna be a big surprise. We get the dough, dump her on the shore and drive the boat upriver. By the time he makes it off the bridge and gets to her, we're long gone. What'd you think?"

"Yeah, it sounds good, might even work, Delton. I see just one little problem."

"What's that?"

"Unless something's changed since the last time I checked, we ain't got no boat."

"Don't you see, man? That's the beauty of this. No one will ever think it's us."

"Huh?'

"We take someone's boat. They won't be able to trace it to us. We grab the cash, and we're home free. Then, we do the same sort of deal with Bono. Not a boat the next time, but something completely different, just as long as they can't trace us."

"Something different? What you got in mind? Not like we can use a plane or a helicopter or—"

"Yeah, look, Clarence, I get what you're telling me. I just ain't thought that far ahead, yet."

"When you planning on doing this? 'Cause far as I'm concerned, the sooner we get rid of her, the better off for all of us, even poor old Bono's about had it, man."

"Yeah, I dig what you're saying. Sooner the better," Delton said and glanced toward the cabin. "While you were gone to the Piggly Wiggly, she just kept bitching. Nonstop. Wondering when the sheets on the bed were last changed. What was the thread count? Can you imagine, who wants to sit there and count threads?"

"Them sheets is almost new. I don't think there's any threads hanging, leastwise, I ain't seen any."

"I'm telling you, she just kept going. Was the coffee decaf? Did we have skin cream or some sort of bullshit? She wanted some cucumber slices to lay on her eyes like that's gonna help you get to sleep. I tell you, she's driving you and me and even Bono nuts. Truth be told, I think we opened his eyes for him. Man's starting to see what a real pain in the ass she is. You saw him get up from the table. Poor bastard just wanted to go back to the bed instead of sitting there having to listen to her piss and moan."

Clarence shook his head. "You imagine all the money in the world, and you gotta live with that?"

"Hey? Hey, you guys? Come mere, please. I need to go to the bathroom now. Hey, did you hear me? Please. I need to go now. Hey."

"Oh, God. There she goes again. We just can't catch a break with that one."

"I'll deal with this," Clarence said and smiled.

"You sure? Don't do anything to hurt her."

"Relax. I'm just gonna lock her in the bathroom."

Clarence stepped into the cabin, noticed there were just two squares of Ex-Lax left on the plate. Sassy was in a semi-fetal position on her chair, softly groaning. She was bent forward with her arms wrapped tightly around her. She looked up as Clarence stepped into the room.

"Ugh, I need to get to the bathroom. I'm, I'm not even sure I can make it. Bathroom. Please."

"Must have been that salad you made me make for you," Clarence said. He knelt down and unlocked the chain from the floor.

"Ugh, bathroom, hurry, hurry."

"Sure thing, let's go."

Sassy groaned to her feet then bent over, clutching her lower mid-section as she took baby steps toward the bathroom. "Oh, God. Oh, God. Please let me make it. Oh, God."

He watched for a moment as she headed for the pink toilet, then closed the door behind her. He heard the explosion a moment later, followed by a loud groan. It all brought a smile to his face, and he walked over to the table, picked up the plate with the two remaining Ex-Lax squares, dumped them into the trash, and headed back outside.

"Everything okay? What was she bitching about now?" Delton said.

"She wasn't bitching about anything for a change. Just wanted to go to the bathroom. I closed the door behind her. Sounds like she might be in there for a while. A long while."

"That figures, now that we're set to get her ass out of here, she decides to stay. I'm telling ya' man . . ."

"I think it might be a good idea if we just give her some space right now. Sounds like maybe all the fruit and vegetables and healthy shit is going right through her."

"Serves her right," Delton said.

Thirty-seven

I studied the two of them through my binoculars. The guy with the beard in the orange t-shirt and his pal. They looked somewhat similar. Brothers? Cousins? Either way, there were two of them and one old rusty car. The odds that this was where Wink and Sassy were being held had just increased. They seemed to be having a casual conversation, and for all I knew, they were discussing getting the oil changed in that Olds or what they were going to have for dinner.

I heard someone shouting from inside the cabin, a woman's voice. I couldn't hear what she was saying, and the voice sounded so shrill there was no way I could tell if it was Sassy. Whatever she was saying, it sounded like an emergency. Maybe she'd fallen, or her hand was caught in the garbage disposal or something. No matter what, it didn't seem to faze either one of the guys standing next to that old beater car.

They exchanged some words back and forth, chuckled, it looked like just general conversation. Then the guy with the beard said something, and they both sort of laughed as he strolled into the cabin, obviously not in any hurry. He came back out a couple of minutes later, shaking his head and carrying a couple cans of beer. They popped the tops on the beer, shared some more laughs, and kept on talking until they finished their beers and went back inside.

I debated about moving up closer to the cabin, but that wasn't going to accomplish anything. One window was covered with plywood from the inside. The other window, with six panes, one of which was covered with cardboard, was right next to the front door. I might be able to pick up something that was said in the cabin, but the chance of getting caught by one of them stepping outside was greater, so I stayed where I was.

Probably a good move. They came back outside a minute later, with fresh beers and laughing. The smaller guy patted the one with the beard on the shoulder, like he'd just done something wonderful. After twenty or so minutes, the bearded guy went in and hurried back out a moment later, shaking his head and carrying two more beers. He said something that kicked off a few more minutes of laughter. They eventually calmed down and just sat there chatting for another half hour before they both went inside. This time neither one of them came back out.

After a couple more hours of sitting there and nothing happening, I was running out of time. I had to get back to the motel and let Morton out. But what would I do if they left while I was gone?

I decided it would be best to eliminate the potential problem.

I crawled forward, slowly making my way from tree to tree until I was alongside the Olds 88. I took my knife out, pushed it into the rear tire on the passenger side, then worked the blade back and forth, slitting the tire. I crawled up to the front of the vehicle and repeated the process. The car slowly began to tilt to the right as the air drained out of the tires. Now, even if they had a spare, they were still going to have a flat. It also meant, whatever I planned to do, I had better do it before they saw the slit tires and were instantly on their guard.

I scurried back through the woods, out to the County road and my Jeep. Other than an assault on my windshield from a couple of birds, everything looked okay. I climbed behind the wheel and headed back to the motel.

Morton began scratching against the door the moment I put my key in the lock. I tossed the tennis ball across the parking lot toward a tool shed. Morton took off after the ball, grabbed it, took a couple of steps, circled, and did his business.

I glanced around, but mine was the only car in the lot, and there didn't appear to be any windows looking out from the office. I tossed the ball again, and again, playing fetch with Morton for a good half hour before I got him back in the room. I refilled his food and water dishes.

I turned the tv on for Morton, then headed back into the town of Dead Fish and parked in front of one of the bars. I got two cheeseburgers to go and drove back out to the cabin. I ate the cheeseburgers in my Jeep, then as

dusk began to grow toward darkness, I headed back into
the woods.

Thirty-eight

The woods were dark by the time I crept close to the cabin. If they had attempted to move the car or discovered the flat tires, I couldn't tell. Four beer cans sat on the hood of the Olds 88 over toward the driver's side, so I figured there was a good chance they didn't know about the tires, yet.

I had just started to move toward the cabin when my cell signaled a text message arriving. I checked my phone. The message was from Preston, so I opened it.

1988 Olds Delta Royale
License registered to Delton Baggott
661 York Ave, St. Paul.
Arrests:
1998 Driving without license
2001 Uninsured vehicle
2005 DUI
2006 Assault
2009 Leaving the scene of an accident
2011 DUI
2011 No Insurance
2011 Car theft

2012 Violation restraining order
2012 Grand larceny
2014 Breaking and entering
2015 Possession
2015 Possession with intent to sell
2015 DUI
Incarcerated 24 months May 2015-May 2017
2018 Charges pending on DUI arrest.
Sounds like a really nice guy. License photo attached. Preston

I clicked on the attached image. A quick glance convinced me, no doubt about it, the license photo was definitely the smaller of the two guys I'd been watching. The arrest record, while not proof positive, moved my odds of being at the right place from 50/50 to more like 80/20. Although, kidnapping was a long way up the ladder from a DUI or breaking and entering.

Another text from Preston came through and I clicked on it.

Battery wearing down so going offline for a bit. Freddy Zimmerman asked about you. Do you know him?

Shit. I phoned Preston. The phone rang a half dozen times, then dropped me into his voice message center.

"Preston, damn it, don't bullshit me about your phone. What did Fat Freddy want? Call me. IMPORTANT!!!"

I waited for Preston to call back, he didn't. I called again and left another message.

"Preston, it's Dev, fucking call me, man!"

After another fifteen minutes, I decided to move up to the cabin and see if I could spot Wink or Sassy.

Thirty-nine

larance shook his head. "I don't know, man."

"That's right, Clarence, you don't know. So, how 'bout this? You don't say shit. I got this all worked out, nice and professional like. Have we had a problem yet?"

"Yeah, now that you mention it. She won't shut the hell up, and she's given you, me, and even Bono, a major league headache."

"I'm talking about the cops. You see any around here? Please, tell me if you do 'cause I ain't seen shit. Everything's going according to my plan, Clarence. We're going to get her out of that bathroom. We ain't heard a sound from in there in the last hour. We'll bring her down to the cities, get the money and be back up here before breakfast."

"You think she's okay to go? I mean, it's gonna be a good two hours sitting in the backseat of your car. Once we get on the Interstate, it ain't like she's gonna be able to step out of the car and have some privacy," Clarence said.

"I don't see as we got any choice. We need to put the pressure on this Hassle idiot, make sure he's got the money. Then, like I said, we drive down to the cities, have him drop the money off the bridge. We put her ass onshore, and we're gone."

"But, Delton, we ain't got no boat."

"I guess you weren't paying attention. I told you, we'll get one. It ain't that big a deal. Hell, she's been in that damn bathroom better part of the day. 'Bout damn time we got her ass out of there. So, you better start moving and get her out of there."

"Me?"

"Yeah, you. You're the dumb bastard gave her all that shit to eat. One of them pieces would have been funny. But the whole damn box, good thing this place has got plumbing and that little window in the bathroom. Now, you go on and get her. I'll get set to call Hassle so we can give him the word."

Forty

I decided I couldn't wait any longer. There were a couple of lights on in the cabin, and neither one of those guys had been outside in the last few hours. I crouched down and began moving from tree to tree, working my way closer to the cabin. I kept my eye on the window next to the door, but the glass was so dirty I couldn't tell if anyone was in there looking out. Fortunately, it was dark enough that I didn't think they would be able to see me.

I made it up alongside the Olds 88, leaned against the passenger side of the car for a moment to catch my breath. I glanced at the two slit tires on the 88, flatter than pancakes. These guys weren't going anywhere.

I crouched down, slowly made my way to the rear of the car and peeked around the corner. Everything seemed quiet, and I couldn't pick up any sort of shadow or movement that suggested someone was looking out the window. I cautiously made my way across the open area toward the front window. I was halfway to the cabin when the front door opened up and the bearded guy stepped out of the door. Fortunately, he was looking back into the cabin, carefully guiding a female figure

with what looked like a pillowcase over her head, helping her as she stepped over the threshold.

"Careful now, just a short little walk, and we'll be
at the car."

"I don't know what was in those chocolates, but
they had the worst effect on me. I must have lost ten
pounds. I hope you're not planning a long drive. Did you
clean out the back seat? There was a mildew odor the
other night."

Sassy. I recognized her voice and nonstop complaints. She was dressed in the same booty denim mini
short shorts and the floral top, only now the floral top
was knotted.

Delton stepped out behind her. I recognized him
from the license photo Preston sent me. No question, it
was him. He was focused on his cell phone.

They were headed for the car. In a matter of seconds, they'd be almost on top of me.

Delton punched the screen on his cell phone, put the
phone to his ear, and said, "Let me make this call and get
dumb ass moving down in the cities."

I had just made it to the rear of the 88, headed for a
clump of trees when my 'Unknown caller' ring tone
went off. It sounded like a rock concert in the Hollywood
Bowl, and I frantically slapped my front pocket hopping
to disconnect the singing ring tone.

**"Unknown caller. Why do you bother? I ain't
never, never, never, never, ever gonna answer you.
Unknown caller. Why do you bother? I ain't never,**

never, never, never, ever gonna answer you. Un-known—"

"What the hell is that?" Delton shouted.

"I see him," the bearded guy shouted. He took two quick steps, dove over the corner of the car trunk, and landed on top of me.

"Uffff."

Forty-one

He rolled off me like a professional football player and, in one swift movement, was up and standing over me. He reached down with his massive paws, grabbed me by the shoulders, and yanked me onto my feet. I was gasping for breath after having the wind knocked out of me.

"Just what in the hell do you think you were doing by our car? Trying to siphon gas?"

"No." I took a deep breath in an attempt to get some air back in my lungs. "I, I was just curious. A 1988 Olds Delta Royale I was looking at it, wondering if you'd ever consider selling it. It's a classic, and I like to restore classics."

Delton sort of struck a pose and looked at me. He seemed to be considering my offer when Sassy pulled the pillowcase off from over her head.

"Dev? I thought that sounded like you, don't tell me you're involved with these two. You gotta be kidding me. I should have known you were up to something."

The brothers looked at one another then at Sassy and finally me. "You two know each other?"

"No," I said.

"Well, yeah. Hello." Sassy said.

"One of you's is lying," Clarence said.

"Of course, I know him. I know everybody," she said and cocked a hip. "I've known Dev Haskell since we were kids in high school, not that I let him date me. In fact, he was supposed to be the security for Bono when you two—" she suddenly stopped in mid-sentence, for once apparently realizing she'd opened her big mouth. "Whoops. Sorry, Dev."

"Wait a minute, Hassle? That was my phone call we heard coming from your cell. I was calling you to tell you to get the money ready 'cause we was gonna give her back," Delton said.

"You bring the money up here?" Clarence asked.

Delton rolled his eyes. "Just ignore him. More to the point, how in the hell did you find us up here?" Delton said then scanned the woods behind me, looking for others.

"Not hard to find you. Thought I'd better come up, take her, and Bono off your hands. Instead of giving you the money, I was gonna let you know you got maybe thirty minutes before the cops come and get you, so you better take off."

"And if we don't believe that bullshit?" Clarence said.

"Then you can wait for the cops. The feds actually, FBI, kidnapping being a federal offense. You'll probably each get a twenty-year sentence and, of course, they tack a fine on. You'll probably be looking at paying fifty thousand or more."

"Twenty years? You shitting me? Hey, Delton, let's get the hell out of here."

"And you're saying we got thirty minutes to take off?" Delton said.

"Used to be thirty, probably closer to twenty by now."

"Dev, who you trying to kid. The FBI doesn't operate like that. I dated an agent for a couple of weekends. Giving two kidnappers a half-hour to run away, that just doesn't sound right."

"Sounds like bullshit to me, too," Delton said as he pointed a pistol at me. "Clarence, see if he's carrying a gun."

"I can save you the trouble, Clarence. It's in my waistband," I said and raised my hands. "Thanks for your help, Sassy. Great move. Really good."

"Well, I was only trying to help."

"Do me a favor, from now on, don't."

Forty-two

elton directed us back into the cabin with a wave of his pistol. I followed behind Sassy, taking in the view. Delton poked me in the back with his pistol, and Clarence brought up the rear.

"Lady, move your ass into the bedroom," Delton said as soon as Sassy stepped into the cabin.

"I would like to say just one thing," Sassy said.

"Oh, shit," Delton groaned.

"You seem like nice guys, so it should be obvious there's barely room for Bono and me on the bed. And I think, under the circumstances, we should certainly be allowed a little bit of privacy. Maybe Mr. Haskell could stay out here in this room with the two of you? He could sleep on the floor. You wouldn't mind, would you, Dev?"

Just keep moving into the bedroom," Delton said.

"Oh, and by the way. I forgot to mention, you're almost out of toilet paper again. Maybe something with a little more cushion this time, that stuff you had was damn near see-through. And as long as I'm on the subject—"

"Will you please just shut the hell up. I can't stand it anymore," Delton said. "Now into the bedroom, and you, sweet cheeks, set your ass down on the chair in there, and I don't want to hear another word. Please. Clarence, get the duct tape."

Sassy entered the bedroom and made a beeline for a wooden chair sitting in a corner. Wink was lying in the middle of the bed. A chain was wrapped around his waist and shoulders. He sort of blinked his eyes open and stared at me with my hands raised. Delton's pistol was still pushed up against my back.

"Dev?"

"Hey, Bono, how's it going?"

"Jesus Christ, what the hell are you doing here. How'd you find us?"

"He wanted to buy their car," Sassy said.

Clarence came back into the room carrying a roll of silver duct tape. Delton indicated Sassy with a movement of his head, then faced me and said, "Yeah, just how in the hell did you end up here?"

"I think it would be best if I showed you. Can I reach in my pocket and get my cell phone?"

Delton gave me a funny look then said, "You just better turn around and face the wall. Assume the position. Put your hands above your head and lean against the wall."

I did as he said, and he kicked my legs further apart, then with the pistol pressed firmly against my spine, he proceeded to search my pockets. He felt the cellphone in my front pocket, reached in, and pulled it out. "Okay, you can turn around now," he said. Once I was facing him, he handed me my cell and said, "Show me."

I ran my finger across the screen, clicked onto my contact list, hit Preston's link, clicked the call button and muted the sound, then brought the text messages screen up, and brought up the driver's license and arrest information on Delton.

"Okay, so here's the information I got on you," I said and showed him the screen.

"Holy shit, where'd you get all that? Facebook?"

"Police and state records. It's all out there, somewhere, you just have to have access, and I do."

"Not so tight," Sassy whined as Clarence wrapped a length of duct tape around her ankles, securing her to the chair. Her hands were taped together at the wrists. Once he had her ankles secure, he pulled a short length of tape off the roll, maybe five or six inches long.

"What are you going to do with . . . Oh no. Now, you just hold on a minute. No, you can't do that, it's going to leave a mark. Are you even listening? I just said you are not—"

Clarence put the length of tape over her mouth then ran his massive paw across the tape, just to make sure. Sassy wrinkled her face in disgust and shook her head as his hand went across it.

"Wrap a length around her head. I don't want her pulling that little piece off and driving us all crazy again. Sweet Jesus, peace and quiet. Finally."

Sassy violently shook her head left and right as Clarence pulled a long length of tape from the roll, tore it off, then wrapped it around her head and over her mouth three times.

Sassy's face grew beet red, and her eyes flashed. At first, I was afraid she couldn't breathe before I realized she was upset from being unable to give direction and complain.

"Thank you," Delton said, then went back to looking at the screen on my cell phone. "Okay, so ya' got all this shit, but that don't tell you where I'm at."

"No, but your cell phone does."

"How can it, I didn't call you? Well, yeah, I guess I did, but that was just a little bit ago."

"And, the other day, when Bono was on the phone. Remember? As long as you have a battery that's working it sends your location up to a bunch of satellites, and that's where I got the information. Long as I have the phone number, I can track you. We all can."

"Who's we?"

"Me. The cops. The feds. Some woman's pissed off husband. Anyone who wants to. That's why I said you guys should probably get the hell out of here. They'll all be here sooner or later."

"And they can track me?"

"Oh yeah, and Bono and the lovely lady over there duct-taped to the chair, along with your brother and me, too. I'm not kidding. You guys should get out of here."

"I think I got a better idea. Hey, Clarence, wrap this wise-ass up nice and tight, so he can sack out with his pal, Bono."

As Clarence stepped over, I slipped the cellphone back in my pocket. Clarence reached down and picked up the end of a long chain and proceeded to wrap it around my waist and shoulders. He padlocked it to the bolt on the floor and guided me onto the bed, next to Wink.

"There, now the two of you's can catch up and not be interrupted." He glanced over at Sassy.

She attempted to stomp her feet, but with her legs taped to the chair, she only succeeded in turning her face red.

"Come on, Clarence, we got some adjustments to make," Delton said, and they hurried out of the room.

Forty-three

I whispered to Wink, "Just what in the hell are you doing here?"

"I wanted to spend some time at the lake, dumb shit. Those two, dumb and dumber, grabbed us after the gig Saturday night. We waited for you outside, but when you didn't show, we headed towards Sassy's car. They pulled alongside and grabbed us. Brought us here. Wherever in the hell this shit hole is."

"At first, I thought it was a joke when you called me. Figured you spent the night with Sassy at her place."

"Yeah, well, I spent the night with her, but not like you were thinking. At least, they haven't hurt us. They still think I'm Bono, and they were counting on you to get the ransom money."

"Yeah, I got a box on my front porch with your vest and a note written by a six-year-old saying a million bucks."

"How in the hell did you find us?"

"I had their cellphone traced, high tech shit."

Wink nodded like that made sense.

"In fact," I pulled my cell from my pocket.

"You're kidding, they didn't grab that from you?"

"You're the one who just called them dumb and dumber. Hang on." The cell was off, so I turned it back on. I phoned Preston again, got dumped into his voice mail, and disconnected. "Damn it."

"Who you calling?"

"The guy who traced the phone that brought me up here. So what's the plan with these two?"

"Good question. You're suggesting there is a plan. I think there might have been one, but that went down the drain when you showed up. They were gonna release Sassy soon as you paid the ransom."

"How am I supposed to come up with a million bucks?"

"Actually, my thought was you would alert the cops, and they'd get us out of this mess. As stupid as these guys are, they've been halfway decent, no abuse, no threats, nothing. Well, other than begging Sassy to shut the hell up."

"What'd she say."

"You name it, bitching, complaining, then she had the shits for the better part of the day. Don't take it the wrong way, but I'm glad it's you next to me in this bed, and she's over there in that chair."

"You sure they didn't hit you in the head?"

"Hey, look man, let's try and figure out a way for the three of us to get the hell out of here," Wink said. "We're chained to the floor in here or in the other room when we eat. They don't chain us in the bathroom, but only because the window is so small none of us could get out that way. When we're done eating, they chain us back up in here."

"It's just the two of them?"

"Far as I know, haven't seen anyone else. The smaller of the two seems to be the brains."

"Delton."

"Yeah, that's the one. Clarence is the other guy. One of the things that bothers me is they put pillowcases over our heads when we drove here, but then they let us see their faces and hear their names. Like I said, they haven't been abusive, but what if their plan was to kill us once they got paid. And now that isn't about to happen, so I don't know. At this point, your guess is as good as mine. Maybe they just head for the hills."

Forty-four

The room was dark, and, with the exception of Wink's snoring, everything was quiet when I woke up. I stretched, then sat up and swung my feet over the side of the bed. I could just barely make out the outline of Sassy taped to the chair. Her head was down, and she was breathing heavily through her nose. I stood and slowly shuffled toward her. I ran out of chain when I was about four feet away. I headed back to the bed and had just laid down when the door opened, and someone looked in the room. A dim light illuminated the area behind whoever it was.

I pretended to be asleep, and after a moment, the door closed. I didn't think I'd made any noise, and I wondered if they had some sort of monitoring device that detected movement in the room.

That struck me as a big leap for these two, but I suppose anything was possible. I drifted off to sleep and woke to Clarence shaking my shoulder.

"Breakfast in a couple of minutes. You're first to use the bathroom. Stay in bed until I unhook your chain."

He stepped back, watched me for a moment, then quickly crouched down, and opened the padlock.

"Okay, sit up."

I did.

"Good, now head for the door," he said. He grabbed hold of the chain and took a step back. "First door on the left is the bathroom."

I made my way out of the room and into the bathroom. Other than some facilities I'd been forced to use in the service, this was, without a doubt, the worst bathroom I'd ever been in, ugly fixtures, a cracked mirror. Fortunately, the toilet flushed. There was a dirt-covered bar of soap in the sink bowl, and I ran water over it until it appeared reasonably clean then washed my hands.

Clarence took hold of the chain as I left the bathroom and directed me to a chair on the far side of a small, crumb covered table. Wink was seated across from me five minutes later, and five minutes after him, Sassy sat down.

Clarence wrapped a length of duct tape around her waist and the chair, stepped back, and said, "I s'pose ya can take that tape off yer mouth. But I'm warning ya." He leaned in closer and whispered just loud enough for all of us to hear. "You start talking, or even one little complaint and Delton's gonna make me put the tape back on and this time it ain't gonna come off. Understand?"

We all nodded.

"Okay then, let me get this off." He began unwinding the length of tape around her head. The first two times around seemed to come off without a hitch, but the third time was a little different. A pretty fair amount of hair remained on the tape, and when she saw it, Sassy's eyes grew wide. She didn't flinch initially as the tape was removed from the side of her face, but then again, she couldn't see the three-inch wide red mark the tape had left. She flinched a little when he got to the front of her face, and then he sped up removing it from the left side of her face. Fortunately, he had the good sense to crumble it all up and toss it in a wastebasket in the corner.

"I'll let you take that little piece off," he said and stepped over to the kitchen counter and pulled three bowls from the cabinet.

Sassy cautiously removed the tape from her mouth, pulling just a fraction of an inch at a time and making little noises as she went. "Umph, ouch, oooh, ufff," then repeating it all again.

Once the tape was removed, Wink quickly put a finger to his lips, signaling quiet.

Clarence delivered three bowls of what I guessed was canned chili and set them in the middle of the table. Wink and I each grabbed a bowl and started eating.

Sassy placed a tiny spoonful into her mouth, winced, wrinkled her nose, shuddered, set her spoon down, and pushed her bowl back towards the center of the table. "Absolutely disgusting," she whispered.

Wink shoveled another heaping spoonful into his mouth then put his index finger up against his lip, signaling Sassy to be quiet.

"I don't care," she said in a loud whisper, then looked over at Clarence, whose back was to us as he ate out of the pan. "That was absolutely dreadful. After yesterday and my reaction to that chocolate, I'm not about to take any chances. It was so disgusting. I—"

This time we both put our fingers up to our lips.

"Well, thank you both for all your support. Not," she whispered, then crossed her arms and sat pouting in the chair like a twelve-year-old.

Forty-five

After the chili breakfast, Clarence led us back to the bedroom one by one. Wink and I were lying on the bed, chained to the floor. Just like before, Sassy was duct-taped to the chair only this time Clarence hadn't placed any tape over her mouth. A perfect red rectangle ran across her face from cheek to cheek, the exact dimension of the tape that had covered her mouth earlier. I figured it would be at least a day, maybe two before it disappeared. Neither Wink nor I had the courage to point it out to her.

Just about lunchtime, Clarence came into the room. He looked nervous. He cut the tape around Sassy's ankles and led her out to the main room. He came back in for Wink and led him out and then did the same with me. We were all seated at the table. Wink and I were chained to the floor.

"Little change of plans here," Delton said, pacing back and forth. "We been talking to some folks, Bono. Your manager and the record company, and they're gonna pay the money. So y'all be free to go. We'll drive you back down to the city. We're going to get started here, and we need you all to stand over there by that wall.

Clarence, you can unlock 'em. You first, sweet cheeks, get up."

Wink shot me a look. Manager and record company? It sounded like a pretty bad lie. Clearly, Delton had no idea what the hell he was talking about.

"Come on, honey, you heard me. Now get your ass out of that chair and stand over by that wall."

"And if I don't?" Sassy said.

Delton pulled a pistol out from behind his back and pointed it at her. "Then, you'll just have to stay here forever. Now move, please. Like a good little girl."

Sassy's eyes began to tear up, and she said, "No, please, please, don't do this."

Delton grabbed her by the hair, pulled her out of the chair, and dragged her over to the far wall. "You so much as move, and you are one very dead bitch."

"Come on, Clarence get . . . now, what the hell is that about?" He said as a long blast from a car horn sounded from outside. He stormed over to the door and tore it open, shouting as he stepped outside. "Hey, just what the hell do you think you're doing? Get away from my car. This here is private property, so just get the hell out."

As Clarence headed for the door, I jumped up from the table and tried to tackle him, but just as I was about to grab him, I ran out of chain. Clarence turned and swung at me, barely grazing my chin, but the tightened chain sent my feet up and out in front of me, so it looked like he had decked me. I landed on the floor with a loud, "Ufff."

Suddenly, Sassy let out a shriek, spun around in midair and slammed a heel right between Clarence's eyes. He staggered back a couple of steps and shook his head from side to side in an attempt to get his bearings just as Sassy bent at a ninety-degree angle and placed a solid kick to his ribs on the left side. She spun around and kicked him solidly on the right side, and I swore I heard a cracking sound. Clarence's right arm automatically wrapped around his midsection. He took a staggering step towards Sassy and reached for her with his massive left paw.

She side-stepped him, grabbed his arm, and, in one fluid motion, yanked his arm, spun him head over heels onto the floor where he sat for about a second before she backhanded him across the bridge of his nose with her fist. His nose exploded, his eyes crossed, and he dropped backward. His head bounced off the wood floor with a loud thunk. She took a half step back and assumed another karate pose in the event he moved. He didn't.

From outside, Delton's voice sounded like he was pleading. "Clarence. Oh Clarence, could you come out here please? Clarence, there's someone here I'd like you to meet. Clarence? Please?"

I took the key from Clarence's pocket, unlocked my padlock, tossed the key to Wink, and headed for the door. Delton was kneeling on the ground next to the Olds 88 with blood streaming from his nose and tears running down his cheeks. The window on the driver's side had a fresh starburst pattern, presumably from Delton's thick skull. Fat Freddy Zimmerman stood next to him, smiling and munching on a chocolate doughnut in one hand while holding a pistol to Delton's head with the other.

"Oh, you are so going to owe me big time for this, Haskell. Big. Time."

Forty-six

We were seated at the table, just Wink and I. Side by side. One of Fat Freddy's thugs was driving Sassy over to my motel room where she was going to shower, wash her clothes, and probably apply makeup for three or four hours. At the moment, Fat Freddy was sitting across from us, taking up the majority of that side of the table. A ring of chocolate circled his mouth.

A white bakery box sat in the middle of the table. It looked like it might have held a dozen chocolate doughnuts at one time. Fat Freddy was in the process of finishing his current pick, which only left three in the box. Neither Wink nor I felt like testing our luck over a chocolate doughnut just now.

Delton and Clarence were outside in the sun, sitting back to back on the ground next to the Olds 88. The chains that had been wrapped around Wink and I were now wrapped around the two of them and padlocked. One of Freddy's thugs was sitting on the hood of the Olds 88, sipping a Special Export beer that he'd grabbed out of the fridge. What looked like a sawed-off shotgun rested on his lap. Clarence and Delton appeared to be deep in thought.

Fat Freddy tossed the last bit of his current chocolate doughnut into his mouth and began to noisily lick his fingertips. Once he'd finished licking, he made a strange face, let out a loud belch, reached in the box, and chose another chocolate doughnut. He smiled and took a large bite. It looked delicious.

"So, let me see if I got this right," he said through a mouthful of doughnut. "Mmm-mmm, at no surprise, you manage to bungle your security detail protecting Mr. Bono, here. You ignore my instructions to stay put. You have Preston track the phone call and decide it would somehow make sense not to let me know. You drive up here to the lake country, where those two halfwits immediately capture you before you have a chance to do anything other than cause more problems. And, in the process, you damn near ruin the birthday surprise Tubby has planned for his granddaughter. Does that pretty much sum up your efforts over the last few days, Haskell?"

"Well, actually, I was concerned with causing Tub . . . err, Mr. Gustafson, a lot of stress and worry. I had hoped to rescue Bono and Sassy and bring them back to the city in time to make the birthday party."

Wink chimed in. "And I'd like to add I'm really looking forward to it. Anxious to meet the granddaughter. How old did you say she was going to be? Fifteen? Wonderful age. I was fifteen once. Had a wonderful birthday. I remember one time we—"

Fat Freddy held a hand up, silencing Wink.

"She's going to love having you, which reminds me. We should get you back. My boat is parked down on the shore. We'll race over to Dead Fish, I'll call my man, he'll meet us there, and we can head back to the city. Haskell, your job will be to make your way to the motel, drive the lady back to the city. Once in town, you'll get cleaned up and bring Mr. Bono to the birthday party this evening. You remember where it's being held?"

"Yeah, Mr. Gustafson's bar on East Seventh, the Reform School."

"Amazing you remembered. And her name?"

"Caroline, no wait, Claudia?"

Freddy gave Wink a long look. "Mr. Bono, I respect your loyalty here, but I've been forced to deal with Haskell for a long time. Do you really think it's a good idea to have him providing your security?"

"I know what you mean, but, ahh, we have an arrangement sort of worked out."

Fat Freddy shook his head, "Must be a hell of a deal. All right. We'll see you at six o'clock this evening, Haskell. That's little hand on the six, big hand on the twelve. Think you can remember? Oh, and Haskell. I'll expect you to keep this morning's activities to yourself. No sense in upsetting Mr. Gustafson. Clear?"

I nodded at Fat Freddy.

"Wonderful. Mr. Bono, we'd best get going, we've one slight delay along the way. Won't take but a minute. Oh, and for the record, Haskell, the birthday girl's name is Cynthia. It would be nice if you had the proper name on the birthday gift you'll be giving her. And you will be bringing a birthday gift. You can change the tires on that bomb out front and get to wherever your dreadful Jeep is parked. See you tonight, do not even think of being late," Fat Freddy said. He carefully picked up his doughnut box and headed out the door. "Come on, Mr. Bono," he called from outside.

"Dev, what the hell do I do?" Wink said.

"Wink, you gotta play the part. Think of it as the academy awards. They find out you're an impersonator. It'll be curtains for both of us. Tubby Gustafson can be one vicious bad guy. You gotta stick to the part, man, for both our sakes."

"Oh, God, okay, okay. I can do this. You'll get Sassy?"

"Yeah, I'll head to the motel as soon as you guys leave."

"Mr. Bono, the ship is leaving. All aboard."

"Coming, coming," Wink called. "Okay, Dev, see you tonight, you're picking me up at my place?"

"Yeah, don't worry, I'll be there."

Forty-seven

I waited next to the Olds 88 until I heard the boat engines begin to roar. I waited another minute just to be sure then hurried down to the shore. With the exception of some birds chirping, the place was quiet. I could see the boat, a large white thing that looked like it was a couple of stories tall, heading at warp speed across the lake toward the town of Dead Fish, leaving a massive wake in its passing.

I watched for another minute or two, and just as I was about to head out to the County road, the boat took a hard right turn sending up a spray of water and stopped. Three of Fat Freddy's thugs wrestled Delton and Clarence to their feet. They were too far away for me to hear anything, but there appeared to be some sort of brief struggle, and suddenly, Delton and Clarence, chained together and kicking, went over the side of the boat and into the water. They splashed around for just a moment or two before they disappeared below the surface of the water. The boat lingered for another minute while the thugs searched the water intently. Laughter drifted across the lake until one of them flashed a thumbs-up signal. The boat seemed to suddenly rise up and race off across the lake toward town.

I waited, watching for a few minutes, but saw nothing. Clarence and Delton never surfaced. I went back in the cabin, recovered my pistol from the kitchen counter, checked the bedroom for anything that might link me, Wink or Sassy to the place, then left the door open and headed out to the County road.

My Jeep was just where I left it, only now there were a half dozen bird splatters on the windshield. I climbed behind the wheel, thought about Clarence and Delton for a moment, and realized there was absolutely nothing I could do about it. I started the Jeep, pulled onto the County road, and drove to the motel.

Forty-eight

Morton was sitting on the sidewalk in front of the door to my room. The moment he saw the Jeep turn into the parking lot, he sprung up and began barking and wagging his tail.

"Hey, buddy, miss me? What did Sassy do, kick you out of our room? Come on, let's see what she's up to. Missed you, pal, sure could have used your help."

I turned the knob to open the door, but it stopped after moving no more than a couple of inches. She had the door latch set so I couldn't get in. "Hey, Sassy, come on, open up. It's Dev. We gotta get going and head down to the city."

"Who's that, Dev? Is that you?"

"Yeah, open up."

"Wait a minute. Let me get something on."

"Oh, you don't have to do that. I won't mind. I'll be the perfect gentleman."

"Yeah, right. You can just forget it. Okay, just a sec."

The door closed, I heard something click and then she opened the door. Her hair was wet from the shower, and she had a white towel wrapped around her. The red area around her mouth where Clarence had placed the duct tape was still visible, but it had faded considerably from earlier this morning, common sense suggested I not say anything. I took a step into the room, stopped, and looked around. Morton followed me inside and hurried over to his water dish.

"What the hell happened here? Did you do all this?"

"Oh, yeah, Dev. Silly me. I just love ripping pillows apart and scattering feathers all over the room. I do it everywhere I go. No, idiot, I didn't do this, your dog, what's his name, did it."

"Morton?"

"I don't know. He's your dog. Is that his name?"

"No, I meant, he did all this?"

Feathers were scattered all over the bed, the carpet, the dresser, my backpack. The place was a mess.

"Are you kidding? Do you actually think I did this? I mean, look at it, feathers everywhere."

"Okay, yeah, I see what you mean."

"God."

"Well look, we gotta get back to the city, fast, so get dressed. I'm going to settle up in the office, and then I'll be back, and we can take off. Shouldn't be more than about five minutes."

"Get dressed? Are you kidding, I've been in those clothes since Saturday night, and today is Tuesday, for your information. That's four days in the same outfit. I washed them as best I could in the bathroom sink, but they're still soaking wet. I can't wear them wet, so take your time, we're going to have to wait until they dry."

Fat Freddy, Tubby Gustafson, or both of them would literally kill me if I didn't have Wink at the birthday party on time. Not something I wanted to look forward to.

"I'm going to go pay my bill, then I'm going to get in the Jeep and drive back to the city. You can come, or you can stay here, but I can't wait for your clothes to dry. I'll be back in five minutes. If you're not in the car I'm driving away, and you'll have to get your own ride back."

"You're kidding, aren't you?"

"No, I'm deadly serious. I have to meet up with those guys who rescued us, and they have, err, Bono. Okay? So please, figure something out and meet me in the car."

I left her standing there, put Morton in the back seat, and headed to the office. The guy stepped out of the room before I hit the bell. I could hear the tv blaring. It sounded like another game show.

"One more night?" he asked.

"No, actually, I'm gonna be checking out. You want to ring me up. I'll pay and get out of your hair."

A smile flashed across his face, and he actually looked relieved. "Have the bill for you in just a second," he said, pushing a couple of keys on the laptop in front of him. A moment later, a printer sprung to life behind him. He pulled my invoice from the tray and slipped two copies out through the opening in the bulletproof glass. I signed off without even looking at the thing, grabbed my copy, said, "Thanks," and headed out the door. Fortunately, Sassy was in the front seat.

Forty-nine

I slid behind the wheel and glanced over at Sassy. She still had the towel wrapped around her.

"Don't even think of saying anything, just drive. And how do I lower the window on this side?"

"You don't need to lower the window. I've got the air conditioning on."

She ignored me and looked at the console. "Does this thing do it?" she said, pushing a button and lowering the window in the back seat.

"Other button."

She raised the back seat window, lowered her window a couple of inches, draped her thong out, then closed the window, wedging her wet thong in place.

"You're kidding me?"

"Hey, I already told you everything was wet, I gotta dry it. So why don't you just drive? Mister I gotta get back to the city."

I pulled onto the County road and headed for the Interstate. By the time I reached the Interstate, Sassy had tilted her seat back and was softly snoring. After how she beat the hell out of Clarence earlier, I didn't dare wake her.

The trip was uneventful, and I pulled in front of her building, a couple of hours later. Rush hour was just starting up. I gently shook her, hoping against hope that the towel might come undone. It didn't.

"Sassy, time to wake up. We're home. Sassy?"

"Oh, wow. We're here already?"

"Yeah, you slept most of the way. Must have really needed it."

"Mmm-mmm, yeah, thanks for the ride, I guess."

She lowered her window and pulled her thong into the car.

"Mmm-mmm, more dry than not. Okay, look the other way."

"What?"

"You heard me, look the other way while I slip this on."

"But I thought, you know, having you meet Bono and all, I thought we sort of had a deal and I could—"

"Yeah, well, our deal didn't include getting kidnapped by those two idiots so you can just turn the other way. Go ahead, look out your window."

I looked out my side window as the traffic passed by. I could hear her struggling to get into her thong in the confines of the passenger seat.

"Be happy to lend a hand if you need some help."

"You just keep looking out that window Mister. Now, let's see, where are my shorts? I put them in the back and— Oh, Dev? What the— Your dog is lying on them. Oh, I can't wear those."

"What? Oh, hey Morton. Come on, get off, boy. Get off."

Morton slowly got up, stretched, then hopped into the far rear of the Jeep. I grabbed the shorts and top he'd been lying on. They were warm from Morton and still damp. "Here you go. I guess they're not quite dry, but at least they're warm."

She took them from me, felt them for a half-second then tossed them back at me.

"That is the absolute f'ing icing on the cake. Remind me never to go anywhere with you ever again."

"Hey, sorry. It's not like I was the one sleeping on them."

"Oh, God," and then she started to laugh.

"What?"

"Nothing. Hey, Dev, thanks. If it wasn't for you, I don't know what would have happened to Bono and I. Probably nothing good."

"Don't thank me. You're the one who knocked the hell out of old Clarence. Where'd you learn how to fight like that anyway?"

"I compete. I'm a black belt in karate, I'm shodan."

"Wow, who knew? One of your many hidden talents."

"Hey, let me ask you something. What's going to happen to those two idiots, Clarence and Delton? Did the police come and get them?"

"Well, no, not exactly."

"What do you mean, not exactly?"

"Well, that guy who was eating the doughnuts. Umm, he was going to deal with it. I think Bono was hoping to keep everything quiet. You know, word of this gets out, there's liable to be all sorts of people who'll want to try and kidnap him. So my understanding is they were going to try and deal with it privately."

"Privately?" She said and then seemed to think about that for a long moment. "But they're going to go to jail, right. I mean, they're not going to get away with it."

"Oh, believe me, they're not going to get away with it. I guess right about, now they've probably already started serving their life sentence."

That seemed to bring a smile to her face. "Okay," she said, then leaned over and gave me a quick peck on the cheek. "Please, don't bother to call me. Ever again. I plan on blocking your number. Maybe I'll see you at a class reunion or something. Bye."

With that, she stepped out of my car barefoot and wrapped in the cheap white bath towel. She hurried into her building and disappeared from sight. The only people who paid any attention to her were a woman who looked about sixty years old and the uniformed building doorman. Their eyes followed Sassy until the elevator door closed behind her. The woman glanced over at me, sitting behind the wheel and just shook her head disgustedly.

Fifty

I showered, shaved, and was just starting to get dressed when my phone rang. Wink.

"Hey, Wink, please tell me you made it home okay."

"Not a problem, we were back in town in about an hour and a half. They had to be doing ninety to a hundred miles per hour all the way down."

"And no one pulled you over?"

"They had flashing red lights on the car. Everyone else pulled over and got the hell out of our way. We just blew past them."

"Flashing red lights? You mean like a cop car?"

"Yeah, I'm telling you, it was really cool. Nice bunch of guys, laughing and joking all the way home. I could have gone for one of those doughnuts, but your pal, Freddy, didn't seem too interested in sharing."

"You were riding in a black Cadillac Escalade, right?"

"Yeah, that's it. You been in it before?"

"A couple of times, but always under different circumstances." I didn't see any point in telling him that was the same vehicle Freddy and his thugs were driving the night they grabbed me in the parking lot of Psycho

Shelia's. I needed him calm, cool, and collected for his appearance at the birthday party later.

"You stay in character all the way to town?"

"Yeah, I think they bought into it. No one ever asked a question if that's what you mean. I pretended to be asleep most of the way."

"They didn't wonder when they dropped you off at your place?"

"Yeah, well, I wasn't sure how that was going to go, so I had them drop me off downtown, at the Saint Paul hotel. I took the elevator up to the top floor, waited five minutes, then went back down and took an Uber to my place. I think they bought it. In fact the guy with the doughnuts—"

"Fat Freddy."

"Yeah, on the way back into town, he thanked me for adjusting my schedule."

"Great. You all set for the birthday gig tonight?"

"Yeah, that's why I'm calling. You said Dumb and Dumber sent my vest to you?"

"Yeah, hang on, let me check. I think it's down in my living room." I wandered downstairs in my boxers, and there the vest was, beneath Morton, asleep on the couch. As I pulled the vest out, Morton half rolled over, but never quite woke up. "Yeah, man, I got it, silver buttons. Right?"

"Yeah, that's it, bring it with you. Okay?"

"Will do. Hey, I gotta bring a gift for the kid. I was gonna stop and get a couple of CD's. Sound okay to you?"

"CDs? You mean like U2 CDs?

"No, hip hop. Yeah, of course, U2."

"Okay, just see if you can get some without Bono's pictures on the cover. Just in case, we don't need a hassle there."

"Good advice. I'll be at your door at exactly 5:30, watch for me. I'm not kidding, Wink. This is like the Academy Awards for the two of us. No screw-ups tonight, we can't afford it."

"Yeah, yeah, I got it."

"Good, I'll be cheering for you. One other thing I should mention, actually a guy, that's Tubby Gustafson."

"He like doughnuts, too?"

"He's Fat Freddy's boss. His granddaughter is the birthday girl. He owns the bar we'll be at and a ton of other stuff. Call him, sir, and don't screw with him. Just yes sir, and no sir, and make sure we get out of there as soon as possible."

"Yeah, got it."

"You, ahh, you hear anything from Sassy?" I said.

"No, and to tell you the truth, I hope I never do. I heard more than enough from her to last me a lifetime. She's a real piece of work. Fortunately, she doesn't have my number or my email. She'll most likely try to contact

Bono, and he'll just blow her off. Major league pain in the ass. You give her a ride home?"

"Yeah, she slept most of the way down. She washed her clothes in the motel room sink, so she just had a towel wrapped around her all the way down."

"Mmm-mmm, you get anything set up?"

"Oh, yeah, I can even give you a direct quote. 'Please, don't bother to call me. Ever again. I plan on blocking your number. Maybe I'll see you at a class reunion or something. Bye.' She got out of the car with the towel wrapped around her and disappeared into her building."

"When's the next class reunion?"

"Wink, I don't think it's an option. Look, I better get moving. I'll see you at 5:30 sharp."

"Don't be late, man."

"Just keep an eye peeled for me," I said and hung up.

I had a tux I bought at Ragstock for fifteen or twenty bucks a couple of years ago hanging in the back of my closet. The shoulders on the coat were kind of dusty, but most of that came off when I ran the vacuum over it. I put it on, pulled out my fancy cummerbund and bow tie, and I was good to go.

Fifty-one

I turned a couple of heads when I walked into the CD store in my tux. People were probably wondering which restaurant I worked at. Thankfully, only a handful of the CD's had Bono on the cover, usually posed with the other band members. I avoided those and grabbed four that had room on the front where Wink could forge an autograph. I pulled up in front of his house fifteen minutes early. He answered about two seconds after I rang the doorbell. He had a guitar strapped to his shoulder.

"Oh, man, you're early. You bring the vest?"

I handed it to him. "I got some CD's you can forge the signature on. What's with the guitar?"

"I'm practicing happy birthday."

"Maybe think about leaving the guitar here."

"Why? Don't you think it'll add something to the deal?"

"First of all, it has a Minnesota Vikings sticker. I'm not sure Bono would do that, he probably has no idea who they even are. And, why make it any more compli-cated. You can just wave everyone around and have them sing along. Fat Freddy said there were going to be a lot of people. The more you have singing with you, the less they can hear you. Know what I mean?"

"Pains me to say so, but I guess you're right."

"Here, unwrap these CD's and sign the things. Now, we're supposed to be there at six. I'm gonna park about a block away and call Fat Freddy, tell him we're coming in, and to get security out front."

"You think there's gonna be anyone out there?"

"I'm almost a hundred percent sure there won't be, but it'll make everyone inside get all wound up. We want to keep everyone happy, especially Tubby Gustafson, but remember, the plan is to get the hell out of there as soon as possible."

Wink nodded. "I like the sound of that, man. I've had enough excitement for one week. I think after to-night, I'm gonna retire the Bono gig for a bit."

That made perfect sense to me. Wink forged the sig-natures on the CD covers using a felt-tipped pen. He had some Christmas wrapping paper and red ribbon that he wrapped the CDs in, and we headed over to the Reform School bar.

I thought it said something about Tubby that he named this bar Reform School, not that I was going to mention it. I pulled over to the curb a block away from the bar. From where I parked, we could see the front door to the place. The only activity was an elderly lady walk-ing down the sidewalk, pulling a little cart behind her with a grocery bag. I called Fat Freddy on my cellphone.

"This better be positive, dumb shit," was how he answered.

"Hey, Fred . . . err, Mr. Zimmerman. We'll be there in about thirty seconds. Can you have some guys waiting out front to escort Bono in? I don't know if there'll be a crowd out there or not."

"Not to worry, he's going to be a big surprise for everyone. Pull up right in front. We kept a spot open for you. I'll be waiting just inside the door," he said and hung up.

"He sound okay?" Wink asked.

"Yeah, he'll be waiting just inside. Apparently, you're going to be a big surprise. When I park in front, you hop out. The birthday girl's name is Cynthia, and just remember, she's Tubby's granddaughter, and we want to get the hell out of there as soon as possible."

"Got it, mate, let's go," Wink said with an accent that at least to my ears didn't sound half bad.

Fifty-two

There were actually two parking spots right in front of the entrance. I pulled in, and before I could bring the car to a stop, a muscular thug with a vicious scar across his chin pulled the door open for Wink and said, "Good evening, sir. Mr. Gustafson is inside, looking forward to meeting you."

"Thanks, mate, appreciate that," Wink said and hopped out of the car. The thug hurried in front of him and led him into the bar. I turned the car off, got out, and followed. A large banner hung over the door;

Private Party No Admittance.

Charming.

Two more thugs, dressed in black suits, stood on either side of the door. One of them looked like the guy who drove the boat that threw Clarence and Delton overboard. He opened the door for me, and as I stepped inside, I managed a weak sounding, "Thank you."

I hadn't taken two steps in the place when I heard a high pitched scream, and the crowd seemed to be surging toward a distant corner of the bar. I wasn't sure if I should run out the door or hide. More high pitched screams, then voices shouting, "Bono, Bono, Bono." Apparently, Wink had been discovered.

I headed towards the crowd. The bar was a horseshoe affair with four bartenders in white shirts and black vests. An awful lot of what looked like fourteen and fifteen-year-old girls in outfits meant for women were jumping up and down, screaming and excitedly waving their arms. I could just barely see Wink in the center of the mob. Off to the side, Tubby Gustafson sat in a black leather wingback chair with a smile on his face and a muscle-bound thug standing on either side of him. He glanced in my direction and summoned me over with a wave of his finger.

As I approached, he said, "Haskell, take a seat." It was more a command than an offer. He pointed to a small wooden foot-stool in front of him. There weren't any other chairs nearby, so I sat down on the stool, it was easily six inches lower than Tubby's wingback chair, and my knees were almost up to my shoulders.

More excited jumping girls and screeches came from the crowd.

"The rumor mill tells me you bungled another operation. Security for that fellow," he said and nodded toward Wink, surrounded by the crowd of girls. So much for keeping a secret.

"Actually, sir. With all due respect, I had things pretty much under control until I was whisked away by your guys. They drove me off, made me walk back to my car, and in the process, Bono and his girl had no security and were snatched. It's a miracle I even found them."

"And an even bigger miracle we found you. Might want to think about counting yourself lucky you aren't treading water like those other two idiots right now."

"Oh, believe me, I know how lucky we were. We were all just glad to see Fat . . . err, Mr. Zimmerman show up and rescue us. Bono wanted to come and make an appearance to show his appreciation to you and Mr. Zimmerman."

"Yeah, my granddaughter is all excited. God, look at them," he said, gazing over at the mob surrounding Wink, young girls still screeching and waving their arms. "You'd think they were dealing with the Beatles."

Yeah, fifty plus years ago, I thought, but wisely didn't say anything. "We're both just glad to be here and able to give your granddaughter a birthday to remember."

He looked at me and nodded, but I had the idea he was thinking of something else. Tubby never let anyone off without first extracting something. "Maybe go to the bar and get a drink," he said. "You look like you could use one."

He didn't have to tell me twice. "Always nice chatting with you, sir," I said, then stood, smiled, nodded, and got the hell away just as fast as I could.

"What'll it be," the bartender said as I stepped up to the bar.

"I'll have a Jameson, no ice. Better make it a double."

"Actually, we're not serving any alcohol tonight, sir. Orders from the top," he said and nodded toward Tubby, sitting over in the wingback chair. "I can get you a Coke, a diet Coke, a Coco-Cola zero, a lemonade, pink lemonade, a root beer, or a Sprite."

"Oh God, I guess I'll have the root beer."

"Would you like the bottle or a glass."

"Bottle will be okay."

Actually, it was okay, more than okay. It might have been ten years since I'd had a root beer, but it was pretty good. After a while, the music started playing, surprise, surprise, U2 songs. Wink danced one, by himself, the only person on the dance floor. He was surrounded by screaming, swaying young girls attempting to shake everything they had. On the second song, he extended a hand and had Tubby's granddaughter join him on the dance floor. They danced three dances together or at least tried to. With all the cellphone cameras flashing, there was a pretty good chance she'd suffer from PTSD by the end of the night.

I wouldn't have picked her out as Tubby's granddaughter, she seemed nice. She was in one of the more conservative outfits of the evening, a cute kid, and obviously thrilled to be dancing with Bono.

At the end of the third dance Wink, said something to her, and she nodded. He kissed her on the cheek, waved to the crowd that was surrounding them ten deep, and wrapped his arm around her for another minute or two of intense camera flashes. He gave me the high sign as he slowly made his way through the crowd and out toward the door.

I caught the attention of a couple of thugs and told them Tubby wanted them to keep the girls in the bar just so no one got hurt out on the sidewalk as we made our way to the car. They held up the hundred or so girls at the door as Wink and I made our way to my Jeep.

I held the door for him as he climbed into the passenger side. "Just get us the hell out of here, Dev," he said as he slid into the seat.

I didn't need any encouragement. I hurried around to the driver's side, hopped in, started the Jeep, and we pulled onto the street. I took the first right turn as a force of habit, so no one could track us. I hadn't gone halfway down the block when a black Cadillac Escalade suddenly raced alongside and forced us over to the curb.

"Oh, shit, Dev. What's this?"

"I don't know. Maybe they just want an autograph or something."

"I don't like the look of this, man."

The passenger door on the Escalade opened, and Fat Freddy oozed out of the passenger seat. He signaled with his hand to roll down the window.

"Hi, Mr. Zimmerman, what seems to be the problem?"

"Leaving so soon, the night's just beginning."

"Well, as you can probably imagine, Bono's pretty beat after the ordeal over the last couple of days. I thought I'd get him back to the hotel. He's got an early flight out of here tomorrow."

"Tomorrow?"

"Yeah, early, real early."

"Well, that just works out perfectly," Fat Freddy said.

"What?"

"Tell you what, Bono, why don't you just get in our car. We've got a great venue, a memorable night set up for you. Come on, you don't want to spend your last night sitting in a hotel room, do you?"

"Actually, nice as the offer is and all, the hotel room sounds pretty good. Like Dev said, I'm pretty exhausted after all the—"

"Seems to me you're forgetting something," Fat Freddy said.

"Forgetting something?"

"Yes sir, it was because of Haskell that you were grabbed in the first place. Now, not to put too fine a point on it, but if it wasn't for us," he glanced back at the Escalade and the unsmiling thugs sitting inside. "Myself, and my associates, well, I think it's a pretty safe bet, you, Haskell, and your lovely lady friend would be about six feet under right now. In fact, earlier today, it looked to me like we arrived just in the nick of time."

"You know, you're right, you did. It's just that—"

"Please, I insist."

"Hey, come on now, Freddy, we've done everything you asked. Tubby know you're doing this?" I said.

"Haskell, one of these days that big mouth of yours is going to get you in some real trouble. Mr. Bono, your carriage awaits," Freddy said and raised his arm toward the Escalade, at the same time exposing the pistol tucked into his belt.

Wink hopped out of his seat and hurried around the front of my Jeep. He shot me a worried look in the process.

As Wink climbed into the Escalade, Fat Freddy raised an index finger at me and said, "You'd be smart just to get your ass home, and stay there, Haskell. We'll bring him back to his hotel." He flashed an insincere smile, turned, and climbed back into the passenger seat.

A thug closed Fat Freddy's door then climbed into the back of the Escalade. Just as the door closed, Wink called out, "Dev?"

They took off down the street. I had to wait for another car to pass before I could pull away. The Escalade took a right at the corner. The car in front of me stopped and then just sat there, not moving.

"Come on, move, damn it," I shouted and leaned on the horn. The taillights suddenly indicated the car was backing up. It slammed into my front bumper, pulled ahead, then went into reverse again. I got the message, more of Fat Freddy's thugs. I sat at the corner for what seemed like an hour, although it was just a minute or two before the car made a left-hand turn and went in the opposite direction of the Escalade. I took a fast right, raced down the street, and never found them.

Fifty-three

The sky was just turning to dusk when I pulled up in front of Preston's mother's house. Through the front window on the first floor, I could see the lights on, which didn't mean much. Preston's mom kept the basement door locked so he couldn't venture upstairs. I ran around the side of the house, opened the coal cellar door, and took the steps down two at a time. The door into the basement was partially open, and I entered the dimly lit hallway and hurried back to Preston's room.

There he was, seated at his semicircular desk, bathed in the blue and red light coming from the three large screens running a cartoon Superhero game. His back was to me, and he'd clearly heard me coming down the hallway, the heels on my dress shoes echoed as I approached, but he didn't bother to turn around.

He kept clicking his mouse and punching the keyboard, not turning around as he spoke, "Hi, you must be Candy, you're early. Be with you in a moment, honey. I'm almost finished here. Go ahead and get undressed, there's wine in the fridge if you want some. Just help yourself."

"I can hardly wait, sexy."

Preston half jumped at the sound of my voice, then spun around in his chair. "Jesus Christ, Dev. I wasn't expecting . . . What the hell are you doing here?" He said, looking me up and down, and making note of my tux.

"I really need your help, Preston. Some guys grabbed Wink and—"

"Wink? The guy that was kidnapped?"

"Yeah."

"Dude, what is it with him? Kidnappers, you, Mr. Zimmerman. Everyone seems to want this guy."

I ignored the question and said, "I'm hoping you can trace his cell. They grabbed him not more than thirty minutes ago. Said they were taking him to some great venue and were gonna give him a memorable night. They gotta be somewhere in town. I've got his cellphone number right here," I said and pulled out my phone.

"Actually, I'm sort of right in the middle of something, and I'm expecting a guest at any moment."

"Yeah, so I gathered, but I'm keeping my clothes on."

"Sorry," Preston said in barely a whisper.

"Gee, maybe I should just hang around, I'd love to meet her. What'd you say her name was, Candy? Hey, maybe I even know her. Tell you what, I'll just go pour a glass of wine for her and one for myself, be nice to spend the evening with the two of you."

"Okay, okay, give me your phone," he said and held out his hand just as a large explosion flared across all three screens, and some creature that looked like a wolf in a black leather vest flew into the sky laughing with a princess looking character tucked under his arm.

"What the hell is that?" I asked as I handed over my cell.

Preston glanced over his shoulder at the screen, "Just gets me in the mood for later on."

"A cartoon? Really?"

He shrugged, took my phone, then spun around and began clicking keys. A map of the US suddenly appeared, quickly hovered in on the Midwest, Minnesota, the Twin Cities, and finally a structure on Salem Church Road in an area called Sunfish Lake. The red dot signifying Winks location began blinking.

"Looks like that's where he is, at least for the time being," Preston said. He clicked some more keys, his printer fired up, and a moment later, he handed my phone back along with printed directions to the address. "Sorry you can't stay, but I know you have to take off. Umm, I'd appreciate it if you didn't mention this visit to Mr. Zimmerman. I'd like to stay on his good side."

"Thanks, Preston, enjoy yourself," I said as I hurried out of his basement.

I raced up the cellar stairs and was met by a reasonably attractive brunette wearing jeans, a t-shirt, and red lipstick that matched her stiletto heels. She held a slip of paper in her hand and was looking a little confused.

"Preston?" she said.

"No, you'll find him down those stairs. Just head down there and follow the hallway into the large room. He'll probably be on the computer."

"God, the things I do for a buck," she said just under her breath.

She sort of rolled her eyes, slung her purse over her shoulder and cautiously headed down the stairs. I wished Preston all success.

Fifty-four

I hopped in my Jeep and raced out to Sunfish Lake. I headed out Highway 52, then up 494 to Robert Trail and from there to Salem Church Road. The area is populated with newer, million-dollar homes spaced out on four and five-acre lots. There isn't an unattractive home anywhere in the confines of Sunfish Lake, one of the million reasons I don't live there.

I once knew an investment banker who lived in Sunfish Lake. He had a palatial estate with a swimming pool, a tennis court, five bedrooms, nine bathrooms, a gorgeous second wife, and a four-car garage. I can't recall what federal prison he was sent to, I think he's got three or four years left on his sentence.

Salem Church Road is a long curvy road with manicured lawns and gorgeous mansions on either side. I spotted the estate before I was close enough to check the address on the mailbox. Cars were parked on both sides of Salem Church Road, and along one side of the curved, brick paved driveway that led up to a portico over the front door.

The expansive front lawn appeared to be trimmed to perfection, and the boxwood hedge along the driveway interspersed with rose trees looked amazing. I pulled over and parked behind a Mercedes. The thing was some sort of sport coup, black with white leather interior and I immediately disliked whoever owned it just because. The top was down, two stemmed glasses, they looked like martini glasses, rested in the console. Since the owner, no doubt figured they were above the law, I guess the martinis were okay. A robin sat on the top of the windshield, taking in the view of all the other expensive cars, and I could only hope he felt the urge to poop before he flew away.

I walked up the driveway, past all the fancy cars, one nicer than the next. There were tags on the windshields, all held in place beneath the windshield wiper on the driver's side. I figured they were probably placed there by valets, but I didn't see anyone who looked like they were attending to parking.

I did see Fat Freddy's Cadillac Escalade resting under the portico. No one was in the car, and there wasn't a tag on the windshield. If this was the party they brought Wink to, it was certainly nice digs. The house was brick, three stories, with white trim and a balcony over the portico. The roof was grey slate, the gutters and downspouts were copper, and the place reeked of money.

I pushed the front door open and walked into a large, round entry room. The floor appeared to be marble. A large crystal chandelier hung in the middle of the ceiling that looked to be about twenty feet high. A wide staircase off to the right side rose up along the circular wall to the second floor. Four gilt-framed oil paintings of old guys holding important looking papers hung on the stairway wall.

I followed the murmur of conversation coming from the back of the house. I entered a massive dining room with a huge table groaning beneath the weight of silver trays piled with all manner of food. Through the leaded glass windows, I could see a crowd of people, all dressed in expensive casual clothes. Lights were strung overhead, illuminating the area. Only three or four couples were standing around the swimming pool, carefully nibbling bits of food. The vast majority of people stood at the far end of the pool, back by the diving boards.

Everyone appeared to be clustered around none other than Wink. Fat Freddy stood next to him, smiling, with his arm around Wink's shoulder like they were best of friends. It seemed the only sensible thing to do would be to load a plate up with food and head outside.

I stepped out onto the patio. Granite pavers covered an immense area around the pool. Trimmed hedges and more rose trees edged the patio. There were a half dozen tables with red and black umbrellas and easily a dozen unoccupied reclining chairs that all looked to be permanent summer fixtures.

As I headed towards Wink and the crowd, I passed a couple who gave me and my tux a disapproving look. She was dressed in a sundress and a pearl necklace. He was in white shorts and a pink golf shirt. The arms on a powder blue sweater were wrapped loosely around his neck. I figured the black Mercedes I parked behind was probably theirs, and for a brief moment, I thought about pushing him into the pool, but took a pass.

I stood at the edge of the crowd and nibbled my plate full of hors d'oeuvres as people shot questions at Wink, and Fat Freddy answered. Women kept stepping in and taking selfies or handing the camera to their significant other and then placing their arm around Wink's waist and leaning in close to rub against him for the photo op. My sense was all of the shots would have Fat Freddy cropped out.

I scanned the crowd but couldn't find any sign of the thugs who had been in the Escalade with Freddy. That struck me as unusual. To my knowledge, he never ventured forth without them, and I couldn't recall a time in the past five or six years when he'd driven himself. But they definitely weren't anywhere in sight.

Fat Freddy kept up a constant patter, giving wise-guy answers to the questions thrown at Wink. If you didn't know any better, you might have actually thought he was a pretty nice guy. At one point, someone shouted, "Why don't you let Bono speak?"

To his credit, Fat Freddy replied, "Recording session in Hollywood coming up and he's not to talk, has to save his voice. He takes hourly gargles of honey and lemon juice."

That brought a lot of ooh's and ahh's from the crowd.

I wondered if Fat Freddy had caught on and knew Wink was a fake, an impersonator? If that was the case, it didn't bode well for either one of us. I'd finished my plate of hors d'oeuvres and was about to head in and load up again when three of Fat Freddy's thugs suddenly stepped out of the house.

I don't think they saw me, or if they did, they didn't acknowledge it. One of them, the thug with the scarred chin, nodded and waved Freddy toward him. Freddy answered two more questions, posed with Wink for a dozen more pictures, then said, "You have all been absolutely wonderful. I know I speak for Bono when I say it's been a real pleasure, hope to see you again soon. And please, keep an eye peeled for the upcoming album. Thank you all, enjoy the evening."

Everyone gave Wink and Fat Freddy a round of applause. They slowly made their way through the crowd, Wink getting a number of pats on the back and a couple of kisses. Fat Freddy just had people stepping out of his way as he waddled back toward the house.

He raised his eyebrows when he saw me and indicated with a shake of his head that I should follow them. We walked back into the house, Fat Freddy scooped up a half dozen fried shrimp in his fist and stuffed them into his mouth as we headed for the front door. We stopped under the portico. Fat Freddy checked behind him just to make sure his thugs were the only others out there with us.

"Perfect timing, Haskell," Fat Freddy said as he wiped his greasy hand a couple of times across the front of my tux. "I'll let you deliver Bono back to his hotel. It's been a real pleasure, sir, thank you for not opening your mouth. Good night, gentlemen."

With that, one of the thugs opened the passenger door for Fat Freddy, and he climbed in. The thug hopped in back, and they were off before the door was closed.

We watched them drive around the circular drive and head out onto Salem Church Road, picking up speed as they went. "You okay, Wink?"

"That guy is absolutely, positively nuts."

"That doesn't even begin to cover it. Come on, let me take you home."

"Actually, Dev. If we stopped for just one at The Spot, it would be okay with me."

Fifty-five

Wink looked at me, shook his head, and said, "What I can't figure out, is that he didn't seem to know anyone there. If he was trying to impress someone, I didn't pick up on who."

"Yeah, the little I saw, he was just talking and glad-handing everyone."

"Far as I know, there wasn't any sort of plan. Who-ever the rich prick is that lives there, he didn't introduce himself. In fact, I never even saw who owned the place. No one pointed him out. Just the usual shrieks of surprise and all the women running over to get their pictures taken with me. Literally everyone standing around listening to Fatty, I never even said a word. And I was ready to Dev. I could have pulled it off."

"You think he knows you were faking it?"

"Honestly, Dev, I don't think he has a clue. He, and those guys in the car, they were planning something as we drove out there, but I couldn't tell you what. I just had the feeling me showing up there was a complete surprise and a distraction for everyone."

"What kind of questions were they asking?"

"The usual bullshit, when's the next record coming out? Why do I wear the glasses? You know, it's funny, but no one ever asks what I'm doing here. It's kind of a universal thought that, of course, everyone wants to come to St. Paul."

"Where'd that bunch of thugs with Fat Freddy disappear to?"

"You got me, man. The guy just wrapped his arm around me and led me into the house. They disappeared, and he just loaded up a plate, and we headed out to the pool. You saw it. We were mobbed for a good forty-five minutes, taking selfies and him answering all sorts of questions. I never answered a one. It was very weird. That's really all I can say, man. Very weird."

Mike stepped in front of us, "Last call, fellas."

"Last call? What the hell time is it," I said then looked around and noticed we were the only ones in the place. "Oh, hey, tell you what Mike, thanks, but we better take off."

"Good seeing you, Dev. I don't think we've met," he said to Wink, then held out his hand. I waited for him to ask a Bono question, but he didn't. "You look familiar, been in here before?"

"My friends call me Wink. I've been in once in a while, but I can't tell you when the last time I was here," Wink said, shaking hands.

"Probably where I've seen you then," Mike said.

We climbed in the Jeep, and I drove Wink home, pulled in front of his place, and put the Jeep in park.

"Thanks for the ride, Dev. Hey, don't take it personally, but if I don't hear from you for a while, it'll be okay with me."

"I feel the same, Wink. Enjoy your retirement from playing Bono."

"Not to worry, I intend to. Thanks again," he said and hopped out of the Jeep. I drove home, and Morton met me at the door. I walked him around the block twice. Once home, I finished the remaining half of the double sausage and cheese pizza in the fridge.

I looked forward to sleeping in and having a leisurely day at the office.

Fifty-six

My cellphone ringing just before 9:00 the following morning woke Morton and me. I was half asleep when I glanced at the incoming number. It looked familiar, but I couldn't place it. I had to clear my throat a couple of times before I answered.

"Good morning, Haskell Investigations."

"Hi Dev, catch you at a bad time?" Wink said.

"Good morning, Wink. I thought the last thing you told me was if you didn't hear from me for a while, it would be okay. Is there a problem?"

"Not on my end. Just wondered if you saw all the posts with a picture of me and about fifty different women from that party I got dragged to yesterday?"

"The granddaughter's birthday party?"

"Well, there's some of those too, but I meant that second shindig, the one out in Sunfish Lake."

"No, to tell you the truth. After the last few days, I was just in the process of getting my workout going, and I haven't had a chance to get online yet. One of those women posted a picture of you?" Morton hopped off the bed, looked at me, and stretched for a long moment.

"Not one of them, more like about fifty of them. They're all over Facebook, and those are just the ones I saw, probably a lot more I'm not aware of."

"Good for you, man. Nice to get out of the business on a high note."

"Well that's just it, all this free advertising, I'm thinking I should keep at it. Maybe this was just the incentive I needed to, you know, make a movie or something."

"Yeah, you could get your picture with your phone number hung in the Ladies room out at Psycho Shelia's."

"Hmm-mmm, I didn't think of that, but not a bad idea."

"I was kidding, Wink. Need I remind you of the last few days? Your kidnapping? What about Fat Freddy Zimmerman abducting you last night? Don't forget Sassy telling you to never, ever, call her again?"

"Not to put too fine a point on it, but that was what Sassy told you. As for me, she would have jumped at the chance for a little more attention. I just needed a break from her constant chatter. But after a night of sleeping alone in my own bed, I don't know maybe—"

"Careful what you wish for, Wink. Anything else?"

"No, just wanted to let you know with all this free publicity, I'm rethinking my decision."

"Well, good luck with whatever you decide, but please, leave me out of it. Nice chatting with you," I said and disconnected.

I followed Morton downstairs and let him out the kitchen door. I put the coffee on, went back upstairs, and grabbed a shower. I was on my second cup of coffee when my phone rang. This time I recognized the number.

"Hi, Heidi, what's up?"

"Hi, Dev, wondering if you can help me. I'll make you dinner, and there'd be a dessert afterward." She drew out the word dessert, suggesting more than just ice cream.

"Count me in, what do you need?"

"You know that treadmill I have?"

"The one in your den with all the clothes hanging from it? The one you haven't used for two years? The one I told you not to buy?"

"Do you want to help me, or should I call the next guy on my list?"

"No, don't do that, I'm in. What do you need?"

"I want it moved out onto the boulevard. I've already printed the sign I'm going to tape onto the handlebar."

"What's the sign say?"

"Free. I just want it gone. And yes, if it makes you feel any better, you were right, it was a dumb idea from the get-go."

"You tell me a time, and I'll be there."

"Any time after six, we're having steaks, you can bring the wine."

"I'll be there, and thanks."

"Just rest up," she said and disconnected.

Dinner and a date with Heidi, telling Wink to count me out of anything having to do with his Bono impersonation, it was shaping up to be a pretty good day, and I hadn't even had breakfast. I let Morton in, filled his food and water dishes, refilled my coffee cup, and made breakfast. We headed for the office a half-hour later.

Fifty-seven

I hadn't seen Louie, but the clues he'd been there were a half-filled coffee mug on his picnic table, and the coffee pot was empty, but the burner was still on. I figured he must have had a court appearance. I'd been sitting at my desk for a while, looking out the window with my binoculars, scanning the sidewalk and the buildings across the street and coming up empty.

A black Cadillac Escalade pulled up to the curb across the street. My heart skipped a beat, fearing it was Fat Freddy Zimmerman, but two guys climbed out and crossed the street headed for my building. They appeared to be reasonably respectable and didn't look like any of Tubby's thugs. I figured they were probably heading for the insurance office on the first floor.

About a minute later there was a knock on my office door, it opened, and the two guys walked in. They wore mirrored sun-glasses, dark suits, starched shirts, and striped ties. I was attired in my Saint Paul Saints t-shirt, white shorts, and sandals. They had neatly trimmed dark hair, and I wondered if they were some sort of federal agents.

The shorter of the two, maybe an even six feet tall, smiled as he approached my desk. His taller pal closed the office door, then leaned with his back against the door and his arms crossed. Morton looked up from where he was stretched out in front of the file cabinet, wagged his tail once or twice, then put his head back down and closed his eyes. So much for intimidating protection.

"Good morning, I'm guessing you must be Devlin Haskell, right?" the guy said and proceeded to sit down on the corner of my desk. His hands looked clean, nails trimmed, no wrinkles on the suit, not the usual sort of visitor I had in the office.

"Yeah, that's me, and you are?"

He shook his head, "My name's really not that important. I've got something here I thought you should see," he said and pulled a cellphone from his pocket.

"Hey, fellas, if you're selling something, I'm really not interested. In fact, I've got a business meeting in just a couple of minutes I'm kind of getting ready for."

"Business meeting," the guy said, then glanced at my binoculars and seemed to study my t-shirt for a long moment. "Yeah, you must be really busy. Like I said, I've got something I'd like you to take a look at. You might find it worth your while." He clicked a button on his cell, swiped a finger across the screen and held the phone up for me to see.

Wink, aka Bono, was all smiles in the picture standing next to a very attractive blonde woman. The photo was clearly taken at the Sunfish Lake party yesterday evening. The one Fat Freddy brought Wink to. I was standing in the background, in the process of inserting what looked like a fried shrimp into my mouth. Whoever took the photo just caught a hint of Fat Freddy's hand on Wink's shoulder. Otherwise, he wasn't in the picture.

"Oh, nice, a photo of Bono. Were you at that party yesterday? Did you get to meet him?"

"That's not the point, but nice you recognize the location," he said and flashed a cold smile. "Our client is in desperate need of having an item returned to them, very desperate need. They would like the item returned in the next twenty-four hours. Be a real pity if that didn't happen."

"Hey, look, no offense fellas, but what in the hell are you talking about?"

"Your pal Bono arrived unannounced, mingled with the crowd, kept everyone occupied. Clever, very clever, actually." He said the name Bono in a way that suggested he wasn't buying into Wink's impersonation. "While you and your friend here kept everyone entertained out at the pool, someone took the opportunity to make off with an item that was very dear to Mr. Gatto. We just think it would be in everyone's interest if it was returned."

"Look guys, no offense, but I don't know what the hell you're talking about. I didn't take anything, and Bono couldn't, he was surrounded by everyone from the moment he arrived until the moment we left. Honest.

Whatever is missing, I think you better check with one of your guests because we didn't—"

"Not listening," he said, shaking his head as he rose from my desk. "I'm going to tell you one more time, while you and your Bono pal kept everyone occupied someone made off with a rather sentimental family piece. The Gatto family is rather upset. But, being good people, they're willing to forgive, as long as it's returned in the next twenty-four hours. Shall we say by tomorrow morning?"

"Guys, honest. I don't have a clue what in the hell you're talking about."

"Then I suggest you talk to your friends in the Gustafson organization. I believe they'll vouch for the Gatto family and the trouble you're liable to find yourself in if it isn't returned by tomorrow."

"Hey, I'd like to help, but could you give me a clue? We talking money, credit cards, or maybe a checkbook?"

He shook his head. "Yeah, sure you don't know. Just get it back. We'll want it tomorrow morning, or our next visit won't be so pleasant. Clear? Oh, and don't think of doing anything stupid like leaving town, that's not going to work."

I nodded, not knowing what else to do.

"Good," he said and headed for the door. His pal held the door open for him. He stopped in the doorway and reached inside his suit coat.

My eyes went wide, afraid he was going to pull out a gun, but instead, he came out with a pen.

"I'll leave you a private number where you can reach us," he said and proceeded to write a phone number on the wall. "I look forward to hearing from you. Sooner rather than later."

His pal closed the door behind them, and thirty seconds later, they were outside crossing the street. When they got to their car, they both turned and looked up at me, staring out the window. The one who'd done the talking pointed an index finger at me as a warning and slowly waved it back and forth before they climbed in their Escalade and drove away. I was too stunned to get their license number.

Fifty-eight

Wink answered his phone with, "Well, Dev, didn't take too long for you to come to your senses and call back. Tell me you're in for more Bono."

"We got a problem."

"A problem?"

I went on to describe the visit I'd had less than five minutes earlier.

"Gatto? Never heard of the guy. Who in the hell is that?"

"No idea. I'm willing to guess he owns that estate we were at yesterday. They wouldn't tell me what was taken, only that it was an item the Gatto family holds dear. Hey, hang on a second, I'm checking that name out on my computer."

I typed in the name Gatto and got fifteen pages of everything from Wikipedia definitions to lawyers' offices. I started scrolling through the pages.

"Hey, you there? You coming up with anything?" Wink asked after a minute or two.

"No, nothing, damn it, and I'm just guessing on the spelling. One or two 't''s?"

"These guys threaten to kill you or beat you up? Were they like those creeps that are always around that fat guy?"

"Sort of, but not really. At one point, when they were leaving, I thought one of them was going to pull a gun when he reached into his coat, but he came out with a pen and wrote a phone number on the wall."

"You call it?"

"Are you kidding? They only left a couple of minutes ago. The whole thing is just weird, they were sort of threatening, or at least, they were trying to threaten. Maybe that's the weird thing, they were trying to, but somehow, I had the sense they weren't about to get physical. I don't know."

"Well, I didn't take anything, you didn't take anything, and I don't think that lard ass—"

"Fat Freddy."

"Yeah, your pal, Fat Freddy. I don't think he took anything. Hell, he was physically attached to me the entire time we were there. We walked in the place, he loaded up on food, and once we stepped outside, we were immediately mobbed by folks. You saw what it was like. He, literally, had his arm around me the entire time, and all the women were taking selfies with me."

A thought suddenly surfaced in my thick skull. "Which of course, stupid me, leaves Fat Freddy's merry little band of thugs. They were nowhere to be seen when I got there, and then they all of a sudden they show up and give Fat Freddy the high sign that it's time to go. I bet it was those idiots. They were probably upstairs rifling a jewelry box, going through purses, or stealing bath towels. Now, I'm going to get hung with this, damn it."

"Dev, what are you going to do? You're welcome to crash at my joint for a while if you need to lay low."

"Thanks, Wink, but I have no intention of getting nailed with this shit. I'm going to have to go to the powers that be, tell exactly what happened, or at least what I think happened. And then beg for mercy from the court."

"You're going to go to the cops?"

"The cops? No, they won't be any help. Technically, we don't even know a crime was committed. Don't get me wrong, I have no doubt, but I don't even know what was taken."

"Then, who you going to go to, your fat pal? He'll probably just tell you to get screwed."

"I just told you, I'm going right to the top, Tubby Gustafson."

Fifty-nine

Wink stepped into my office forty-five minutes later, he was in his Bono outfit, wearing the Bono glasses, all dressed in black and his vest with the silver buttons. I was on the phone, listening to Tubby Gustafson's recorded message telling me I'd reached a private number, and I could leave a message after the tone. The recording had an official sounding female voice and never mentioned Tubby by name.

"You have reached a private number. Please, check the number you dialed. If you wish to leave a message, you may do so after the tone, and we will review your message."

"Yes, Mr. Gustafson, this is Dev Haskell. I thought you should know, I had two visitors this morning who mentioned you and did not sound all that happy. Please, call me," I said and left my number.

"Think he'll call you back?" Wink said, when I tossed my cellphone on top of a stack of files. He'd sat down in one of the client chairs in front of my desk, the chair with the duct tape.

"It's the third message I've left since I talked with you, and he hasn't bothered to answer the first two, so no, I don't think he'll answer."

"So why are you—"

"Because I can't think of what the hell else I should do. Whatever it was that was taken, these guys said they wanted it back by tomorrow morning." I checked the time on my cellphone. "It's already after ten, I've barely got twenty-four hours to come up with something. So what's with the Bono clothes?"

"Thought you might need some help, and we can probably get more answers and faster if I'm dressed like this and play the part."

"Wink, that's very kind of you, but I'm starting to get a bad feeling about this, and I don't think you should get involved. I'm afraid this is going to get ugly, really ugly."

"You mean with those guys that paid you the visit?"

"Yeah, but they're not going to be a problem until tomorrow. Right now, I'm just thinking, let's say for the sake of discussion that one of those idiot thugs did steal something from that soirée out in Sunfish Lake yesterday. If that's the case, I would guess it's probably logical that all of those guys are involved. So, when I put the pressure on, I become the problem. You see? Soon as I talk with Tubby, tell him what happened, I'm gonna be their target."

"Target?"

"Once we find out who took whatever it is that's been stolen. We have to accuse him."

"So, won't they just give it back?"

"Maybe you or I would, but these guys aren't normal. Once we accuse someone, he's going to deny it, he'll have to, and we, or I, become a problem he's going to want to eliminate. That's why I'm hoping to go from the top down and talk to Tubby first. But time is of the essence, because the other thing that might happen, the guy who took it, decides to unload it. He could fence it, pawn it, sell it, or even throw it in the river, and then come after me. Sort of like a lose-lose proposition."

"So, what are you going to do?"

I picked my cellphone up from the desk and hit redial again.

After two rings, I got dumped into Tubby's message center. "You have reached a private number. Please, check the number you dialed. If you wish to leave a message, you may do so at the tone, and we will review your message." I disconnected and set the phone down.

"No answer?"

"Oh, no, actually, he answered, but I decided I didn't want to talk to him right now."

"What?"

"Joking, Wink. It's the same damn recording. I don't know, I think—" My phone rang, interrupting what I was going to say. The incoming number was listed as Tubby.

"Haskell Investigations."

"Please, hold for Mr. Gustafson," a very feminine sounding voice said. I couldn't tell if it was live or a recording. I shrugged my shoulders at Wink and kept the phone up against my ear. It was another five minutes before Tubby came on the line.

He coughed and hacked into the phone for a good thirty seconds, then sounded like he cleared his throat and spit before he said, "What is it this time, Haskell?"

"Thanks for taking my call, Tub . . . err, Mr. Gustafson. I've run into a bit of a problem, and I just wanted to make you aware of it, so you're not blindsided."

"A problem. You know how I hate problems, Haskell. What in God's name have you done now?"

"Actually, nothing, sir. This came out of the blue, although I think it might be related to someone on your staff."

"What the hell are you talking about, and if you tell me one of my granddaughter's friends groped Bono last night and he's going to sue, you'd better think twice."

Sixty

We were in my Jeep, heading over to the East side of town. "Where'd you say we were going?" Wink said.

"Magic Moments, that's where Tubby is. Said he wanted to talk to us in private."

"Sounds like a toy store."

"In a manner of speaking. He's there at least three times a week that I know of. I think he owns the place, but I don't know that for sure. I tried to find out online once, but I could only go back as far as three shell company names. I know he owns the building, and he doesn't like to share. So, it would be a pretty safe bet he owns the business, too."

I took a left off of East Seventh onto Payne Avenue, drove another four blocks, and pulled over. Magic Moments occupied the two-story red brick building on the corner. At the top of the building was a granite stone with the date 1875 carved into it. With the exception of the red neon sign flashing Magic Moments, nothing on the exterior suggested the building had been updated in the last hundred and forty-plus years.

"Okay, Wink, I'm going to tell you again, you don't have to come in with me. In fact, I think it's a bad idea if you do. He finds out you're not Bono, and that you pulled a fast one on his granddaughter, we're both liable to end up on the bottom of the river wrapped in concrete blocks before sunset. This guy is one vicious bastard."

"Thanks, Dev, but I feel like I owe you. Because of you, my Bono gig really took off. I still don't know if I'm going to stick with it, but it's nice to have an option. So, I'm going in. Besides, he seemed nice enough yesterday at the birthday. Maybe he just likes me better. You ready?"

"As ready as I'll ever be. Just let me do the talking, okay? He has a tendency to go off on tangents, and over the years, I've found the best response to be a simple, yes sir."

"Sure, sure, not a problem," Wink said and climbed out.

We walked into a small office with a half dozen leather chairs pushed up against the far wall and a large woman who looked about sixty sitting behind a receptionist counter. The place had the smell of cinnamon-scented incense.

The woman behind the receptionist counter flashed a fake smile for just a second and said, "Welcome to Magic Moments, gentlemen. How may we pleasure you today?"

"Actually, we're just here to see Mr. Gustafson. He's expecting us."

"Your name, sir?"

"Haskell, Dev Haskell."

"And sir?" she said, glancing over my shoulder.

"Just tell him, Bono," Wink said, using his accent.

She ran her fingers across the computer keyboard. After a moment, she looked up and flashed another fake smile. About ten seconds later, a beep sounded on her computer. She read the screen and said, "Just through that door, gentlemen, they're expecting you."

She pointed to what looked like a solid steel door. As we approached, a buzzer went off, and I heard a lock snap on the far side of the door. I pulled the door open and stepped into a hallway. The walls were painted an off white, there was beige carpeting the length of the hallway, and it was very quiet.

A woman in a very short red silk robe with white trim stood by an open door a little way down the hall. She looked to be late twenties, maybe thirty and very attractive.

"In here, gentlemen," she said, then stepped aside as we approached and entered the room. There was a wooden bench, and maybe a dozen lockers lined up against the far wall. She smiled and said, "You can store your clothes in a locker. You'll find a towel in there, wrap the towel around your waist, and join me out here in the hall. As soon as you're ready, I'll take you to the shower room."

"There might have been a little misunderstanding, as nice as they are, we weren't going to partake of your services. We're actually here to speak with Mr. Gustafson, at his request. My name is—"

"Yeah, I know, you're that Hassle guy, and you, you're Bono," she said and held her hand out to Wink. When he took her hand, she moved in close and said, "No charge for you today, Bono. Anything you want, it's absolutely free. Anything at all." She stepped back and looked at me. "Mr. Gustafson insists that anyone who meets with him here be properly attired, namely a towel and nothing else. No exceptions. As soon as you're ready, you can shower, and then I'll take you to see Mr. Gustafson. I'll wait for you out in the hall."

She smiled, stepped out into the hall, and closed the door behind her.

"You gotta be kidding me. We're supposed to see this guy with our clothes off?" Wink said.

I opened a door on one of the lockers and said, "Think about it, man. They probably have a monitor on us right now. If we were here to do him any harm, it would be pretty tough to sneak a weapon in. We hit the shower, they'll search the towels to make sure we aren't carrying. It's actually a pretty good safety measure."

I clicked on my phone and checked the time. "It's almost noon. I don't have all that much time left before those two guys come back looking for me, and I've got a very unpleasant feeling they're not going to be as nice as they were this morning. So, seeing Tubby and just wearing a towel is the least of my problems." I pulled my t-shirt off and hung it on a hook in the locker, un-buckled my belt, and looked at Wink. "Come on, man, in for a penny in for a pound."

He seemed to think about that for a moment, then opened the locker door and hung up his vest.

"There, now, that wasn't so bad, was it?" The woman in the red silk robe said once we stepped into the hallway. She moved closer to Wink, who was still wear-ing his Bono glasses. "Let me show you where to go," she said, wrapping her arm around Wink and heading down the hall, I followed. She stopped in front of a door and looked at me.

"Mr. Hassle, you can just shower in here. When you step in the shower, an automatic timer will turn on the water. You can adjust the temperature to your liking, but please, remain in the shower until the water stops run-ning. It's not quite five minutes. Dry off and wait. Once I knock on the door, you can come out, but not before."

As I opened the door into my shower room I heard her say, "Bono, I was thinking of a little special treat. I'm sure you'd like your back scrubbed."

My shower room was small, with a tiled floor and a wooden bench attached to the wall. A couple of wooden pegs were on the wall above the bench. I hung my towel on one of the pegs then opened the shower door. The water immediately started running. I adjusted the tem-perature and stepped in. The glass walls of the shower stall immediately steamed up. I stood there for what felt like a long time before the water stopped. I stepped out and noticed that my towel was hanging on the opposite peg from where I was sure I had placed it. I dried off, wrapped the towel around my waist, sat down and waited, and waited some more. Finally, there was a knock on the door, and it opened.

"All set, Mr. Hassle?" The woman said. Her hair was wet, her face was flushed, and her red silk robe appeared completely dry, although now it was incorrectly buttoned. Wink was standing in the hallway with his towel wrapped around him and a large grin on his face.

"How was your shower?" I said.

"Best one I ever had."

"Gentlemen, if you'll follow me, Mr. Gustafson will see you now." She led us down a hallway then knocked on a door. She said something to the thug who opened the door, stepped aside, and indicated we should enter.

As I stepped in, I heard Wink whisper, "Thank you."

"Oh, believe me, my pleasure," she whispered back and ran her hand across his shoulder as he entered the room. Once inside, the thug closed the door behind us.

He was dressed almost the same as we were. Just a white towel wrapped around his waist and, as sort of an accent on his attire, a brown leather shoulder holster with two additional ammunition clips under his right arm. What looked like a 1911 .45 with wooden hand grips holstered under his left arm.

"All right, fellas. I gotta check you, so drop the towels and spin around slowly, one at a time."

I tossed my towel on a metal folding chair against the wall, raised my hands in almost a surrender position, and slowly turned around. "Like the view?"

"Not really. Okay, you next, sir," he said to Wink.

As Wink turned around he said, "You get paid extra for this?"

"God only knows, I should. Okay, thanks, grab your towel, and Mr. Gustafson is on the other side of that door. It's a pleasure to meet you, Mr. Bono. I dig your music."

Wink smiled and held out his hand, "Don't think I caught your name."

He just looked at Wink's hand and said, "I don't think I gave it."

Sixty-one

The view was unpleasant, to say the least. Two well endowed, attractive looking Asian women stood on either side of a massive reinforced massage table. They were both wearing small thongs and big smiles. Splayed out, face down on the table in all his corpulent splendor was none other than Tubby Gustafson, all three hundred plus pasty white pounds oozing over the edge of the table.

The women, working in tandem, were kneading the flesh on his back. They each wore a pair of blue latex gloves. No doubt, protecting their hands from germs the Center for Disease Control had probably yet to encounter. I thanked God for small favors because a large towel covered his massive rear end. I could see the sides of his stomach hanging over the edge of the table and jiggling as they worked back and forth across his well-upholstered shoulders.

We stood there for what seemed an eternity until I finally said, "Sorry to interrupt, Mr. Gustafson. I wanted to thank you for taking the time to see us this morning, sir."

He kept his eyes closed, didn't move his head, and said, "And I'd like to remind you that you're interrupting my meditation session. The one bit of relaxation I get during any given day, and here you are, Haskell. Imagine my surprise." He exhaled loudly and said, "Well, I'm ready. Exactly what was so important that it couldn't wait?"

"Well, sir. You remember Mr. Bono here. He was kind enough to attend your granddaughter's birthday yesterday. Lovely event by the way and what a charming young lady. I was—"

Tubby opened one eye and glared at me. "I thought I gave you very specific instructions not to go anywhere near my granddaughter. Not to talk to her, not to acknowledge her, and certainly not to touch her.

"Yes, sir, you did, and I followed your instructions to the letter, sir. I just happened to be able to see her from a distance, and she seemed to be a lovely young lady."

"You just remember to keep your distance."

"Yes, sir, believe me, I will. Actually, sir, it was Mr. Bono here, who commented on how nice and polite she was."

"Oh, yeah?" Tubby said, opening both eyes. "Bono, I want to thank you for making the appearance. It meant a lot to Cynthia. Sorry you couldn't have stayed a little longer and had to rush off after such a short time. Didn't you say you had a recording session scheduled out in Hollywood or somewhere today?"

Wink shot me a look.

"Well, sir, that's why we wanted to talk to you. You see, yesterday—"

"Haskell, silencio. I've no need to hear whatever you're about to say. I'm sorry, you were about to say, Bono?"

"Well, yeah, I mean, yes sir. See once we left the wonderful, gracious soirée you put on for your granddaughter—"

"Apparently, my little princess has pictures up on Book Face, YouDude, and InstaCam, or whatever those places are called. So, thanks to you, I'm quite the hero in her eyes. At least, for the moment."

"Wonderful, sir. You're so very lucky to have her. But after that charming affair, I was taken to another event by some members of your staff. Very nice, lovely people, although there seems to have been a bit of a problem and—"

"Hopefully, you enjoyed yourself."

"Yes, sir. Very much so. However, as I just mentioned, there seems to have been a bit of a problem."

"Problem?" Tubby immediately raised his head, looked at me, and half-shouted, "For God's sake, Haskell, now what? Exactly how in the hell did you manage to somehow screw things up on my granddaughter's birthday?"

The two women appeared to put some extra effort into working his plump shoulders and the folds around his fat neck. He gradually calmed down and placed his red face back on the small pillow, closed his eyes, and let loose with a little fart.

"So, tell me, Haskell."

"It was an event with a lot of people standing around a swimming pool. All sorts of women taking selfies of themselves with Bono. Your aide, Mr. Zimmerman, was helping Bono, answering questions for him so he could rest his voice. But then this morning, two men came to my office and told me that an item was missing from the home. Something the family holds very dear. They did not appear to be too happy, and they said I have until tomorrow morning to return the item."

"And exactly why am I having my daily meditation interrupted?"

"Well, sir, I, or rather we, were hoping you might check with your staff to see if perhaps, maybe someone, inadvertently picked something up and forgot to return it. Sort of."

"And do you have any idea who these two gentlemen were this morning?"

"I believe their name was Gatto."

Tubby opened his eyes and raised his head. "Gatto? Faustino Gatto's grandsons?"

"I don't know that, sir. I wasn't familiar with that name or them."

A disgusted look appeared on Tubby's face. He stared at me for a long moment before shaking his head. He exhaled loudly and said, "It never fails, Haskell. Once again, you've managed to ruin the moment. All right, it's clear I'm not about to get any rest here today. Give me thirty minutes and wait in the lobby. I'll send someone for you. Go on, go, go," he said and waved a blubbery arm shooing us out the door.

As we left, he attempted to roll over onto his back. The reinforced table started to creak and rocked back and forth. "I'm feeling a need to relieve some stress," he said to the women suffering through his massage.

Sixty-two

It was close to an hour before someone came and got us. Once dressed, we were escorted out to the lobby where we sat and stared at the bare wall as the clock behind the receptionist counter slowly ticked off the seconds. The same guy who'd had us pull our towels off and spin around in front of him finally rescued us from further boredom.

The steel door made its buzzing sound, and we heard the lock snap just before he opened the door. At least, this time, he was dressed, although his shoulder holster was still clearly visible. "Gentlemen, if you'll follow me, Mr. Gustafson will see you now."

I had to shake Wink awake. We walked back through the security door and down the hallway, traveling all the way to the end of the hall, where a small elevator brought us up to the second floor.

Once the door opened on the elevator, our escort said, "Down the hall, first door on your left. Knock, wait a moment, and go in." We stepped off the elevator, and he followed us down the hall.

The door was painted bright red. A black Chinese character edged in gold was attached to the door. I knocked softly, waited a moment before I cautiously opened the door, and we stepped in. Our escort closed the door behind us and stood in a corner.

Tubby was seated at a round table. A white linen table cloth was draped over the table and hung almost to the floor. A woman sat on either side of him. I think they were the same two women who had been giving him his massage, but I couldn't be sure. They were dressed now, and they weren't wearing blue latex gloves. They appeared to be taking turns cutting bitesize pieces from a large steak on the platter in front of Tubby and then feeding the pieces to him.

Fortunately, Tubby was dressed. He had a linen napkin tucked under his chins. As we approached, he signaled the women to stop feeding him with a wave of his hand. He didn't bother to look at us. Instead, he reached across the table and took hold of a large wine glass filled with red wine. He moved the glass in a circular motion for a moment, shoved his big fat red nose into the glass until it was just a fraction of an inch from the wine, and noisily sniffed the bouquet. He took a large gulp that emptied half the glass. He set the glass on the table, and looked at us, oblivious to the drop or two of red wine that ran down the side of his chin and dripped onto the linen napkin.

"Haskell, I believe you were telling me about the visitors you had this morning."

"Yes, sir, there were two guys. They told me an item was missing that was very dear to the Gatto family and that if I mentioned it to your organization, you would vouch for them and the trouble I would find myself in. I don't know anything about the Gatto family. I'm not sure I've ever even heard of them."

"Describe these men to me."

"Like I said, there were two of them, one maybe six-two and the other an even six feet. I guess they could have been late thirties, maybe early forties. They looked somewhat similar, nicely dressed, neatly trimmed dark hair. They wore mirrored sunglasses so I couldn't see their eye color. They were dressed in suits and starched white shirts. To tell you the truth, they looked more like high priced attorneys or maybe investment bankers instead of gangsters. But, I have no reason to doubt the message they were giving me."

"This, this incident was supposed to have happened where?"

"Well, once we left your party, sir, we drove around the corner and Fat, err . . . Mr. Zimmerman stopped us and had Bono join him in his car. I was able to track them to a large home out in Sunfish Lake. I drove—"

"On Salem Church Road," Tubby said and almost smiled. He got a faraway look in his eyes and said, "Faustino Gatto. I'll be damned. And yesterday, of course."

He took another noisy gulp of wine, and we waited. Finally, I said, "I'm afraid I'm not quite following, sir."

"Faustino Gatto, a giant in his time. You might say he was my mentor. Took a shine to me. If it wasn't for him, well, I sure as hell wouldn't be here today."

He nodded at the woman to his left. She quickly cut a piece of steak and fed it to him. He chewed for a moment then said, "Mmm-mmm, and did they mention the item to you?"

"Not in so many words, sir. Only that it was very dear to the family and needed to be returned by tomorrow morning."

He nodded as if this made perfect sense. "I'm willing to wager it's a diamond necklace, the DeBeers Lizzie Lape necklace, as a matter of fact. One hundred and eighty-one carats in diamonds with a large eight carat stone in the center, if I remember correctly. Very nice, if I do say so myself. Of course, it's dear to the family. I was the one who gave it to their grandmother back in nineteen sixty-nine."

"It sounds lovely, sir, and how very generous of you. But, apparently, now it's missing, and somehow they think I can get it back."

"And why, exactly, did they bother to waste their time with the likes of you?"

"They had a cellphone picture of Mr. Bono and Mr. Zimmerman, and I was in the background. We were all standing out by the swimming pool at that Sunfish Lake mansion for maybe the better part of an hour while all sorts of women took their pictures with Mr. Bono and asked him questions. Mr. Zimmerman spoke for Mr.

Bono, for most of the time, and then, the men who had driven Bono there suddenly came out of the house, gave them a nod, and we left. I drove Mr. Bono home, err, that is, back to his hotel and thought nothing of it. I don't mean to accuse, sir, but it would seem to me there is a good possibility that maybe, just maybe, one of the men who had disappeared for a half hour or so may have mistakenly hung onto the necklace and left, forgetting to return it."

"And what's your version, Bono?"

"Pretty much the same, sir," Wink said. "It was a very lovely home, and Mr. Zimmerman kept his arm around me the entire time we were there. For safety's sake, I'm sure," Wink quickly added. "Just like Dev said, the driver and his two friends stepped out of the house after about thirty minutes, gave us a nod, Mr. Zimmerman grabbed some more shrimp, and we all headed out to the cars."

"Mmm-mmm," Tubby mumbled. He took another large gulp of wine, this time keeping his potato-sized nose out of the glass and said, "Satan, fetch my cellphone."

The thug who searched us earlier hurried out of the room. We stood silently and watched as the two women fed pieces of steak to Tubby for the next few minutes while we waited for Satan to return. He hurried back into the room, placed the cellphone on the table in front of Tubby, then stepped back and stood behind Wink and me.

Tubby drained his wine glass, gave an exasperated sigh, swiped a fat finger across the phone screen, and pressed a button. "Haskell, if only I had a dollar for every day you've ruined," he said, shaking his head. "I'd be able to—yes, Freddy, sorry to bother you. Seems to be a problem and I'd like you to fix it. Quickly."

Freddy said something I couldn't hear. Tubby shook his head, pulled the linen napkin with the wine stains out from beneath his chins, and tossed it onto the table.

"No, not that, at least, not yet. No, apparently there was some attendance by parties unknown at the Gatto family residence yesterday. I believe you were there, as well, chaperoning Mr. Bono. It would have been the anniversary of Fastino's passing." Freddy responded, and Tubby gave a disgusted look. "No, they do it every year, on the day. I would have attended, were it not for Cynthia's little birthday celebration. I sent my condolences. I'd like you to assemble everyone who was there and meet me at the country retreat. No, I don't want to wait that long. This is quickly becoming personal," Tubby said as his facial complexion began to quickly grow red. "The problem? Well, apparently, something is missing. An item I'm intimately familiar with, and that the family holds dear. I'd like it returned, immediately. I'll expect to see everyone in two hours. Thank you," he said, disconnected, tossed his phone onto the table, and then shook his head as a frighteningly evil look drifted over his face.

One of the women began to cut his steak, but he waved her off with his hand.

"Once again, Haskell. At no surprise, you seem to have ruined my appetite, not to mention my day. I want you to return to your office and await further instructions. Mr. Bono, I think it might be best if you caught the next flight to Hollywood for your recording session. Enough, now, both of you, be gone," he said and reached across the table for the bottle of wine. He filled his glass almost to the brim.

Satan, the thug behind us, opened the door and signaled with a nod of his head that we should leave the room. I didn't have to be told twice. Past experience had taught me not to say a word, but just to get out and as far away as fast as possible while I had the chance. Tubby's face had grown three shades redder, and someone, somewhere was going to pay the price. I wanted to be sure it wasn't Wink or me.

No one said anything on the elevator on the way down to the first floor. Satan led us down the hallway, pushed the button that buzzed, and unlocked the door then slammed the door closed behind us the moment we stepped into the lobby.

"Hope you had a pleasant experience," the woman behind the receptionist counter said and flashed another fake smile for a brief second.

We just hurried out the door.

Sixty-three

As we stepped out of the building, Wink said, "Can you please, explain to me what in the hell is going on? You pick up on that pissed off look your pal Tubby had?"

"Yes, I did, and I'll explain once we're in the car and safely on our way. Come on, let's get out of here while we still have the chance."

We hurried into my Jeep. I waited for the traffic to pass, then made a U-turn in the intersection and sped back down Payne Avenue. "Okay, so here's what I picked up. Tubby thinks a diamond necklace was probably stolen. Just the brief description he gave, a hundred and eighty-one carats in the thing—"

"Plus, an eight carat stone."

"Yeah, that too, makes it sound like it's out of my price range. He gave it to this Faustino Gatto guy's wife back in sixty-nine. God, Tubby couldn't have been more than twenty, if even that."

"Where does a guy that young even get the kind of money needed to buy a necklace like that?"

I looked at Wink. "Wink, try and follow along here. He didn't buy the damn thing."

"Well then how in the hell does he . . . Oh, yeah, I s'pose. Yeah, that would work."

"Yeah, you think? So, anyway, he steals it and gives it as a gift to this Gatto guy's wife. Her husband apparently was Tubby's mentor. I don't know this, but I'm guessing the gift of the necklace sort of locks Tubby into the family business. Maybe, it makes him the heir apparent for all I know, which leads to his future success, and right now, he's one pissed-off bastard."

"You think he'll find out who took it?"

"I got a feeling he already knows, and I'm just glad it ain't me. Whoever it is, they're about to pay one hell of a price."

"So, now what?"

"Well, I'm going to do as I'm told. I'm gonna go back and sit in my office and wait for Tubby, or Fat Freddy, or some other idiot to stop by and give me further instructions. If I were you, I'd take Tubby's advice and get on the next flight to Hollywood. Maybe, stay out there for a week or two."

"You mind maybe dropping me off at home, first. I don't really feel the need to see these guys ever again. I'll pack a bag and disappear for a while."

"Not a problem, believe me, I get it. Say, you might want to think about giving the Bono bit a break for a while, at least until things quiet down. No telling who might post something, and suddenly, your location is out there for everyone in the world to see. "

"Yeah, good advice. But Mr. Gustafson knows we didn't have anything to do with this, right?"

"Yeah, I think he knows, but collateral damage is always a possibility with these jerks. So it'd be a good idea to play it safe and give Bono a rest. He finds out you fooled him on the gig with his granddaughter, no telling what might happen."

Wink nodded and said, "No offense, Dev, I mean it's been great seeing you, really it has. You know, re-connecting, having some laughs, helping to save Sassy and me and shit. So, please don't take this the wrong way, but if I didn't hear from you until our next class reunion, that'd be okay." Fortunately, Wink followed up with a laugh.

"No offense taken, Wink. I kind of feel the same way."

We didn't speak the rest of the way until I pulled in front of Wink's place. We shook hands, said something nice to one another, then Wink hopped out of my car, and hurried up to his front door without looking back. I had the feeling he couldn't get away from me fast enough.

I drove down to my office and parked across the street. When I opened the office door, Morton was asleep in front of the file cabinet, and Louie was paging through a file with his feet up on his picnic table desk. He casually looked over at me as I stepped in.

"Well, there you are. I was beginning to wonder. Business?"

"More like pain in the ass work." I went on to explain the last few hours to him.

When I was finished, he seemed to think for a moment and said, "You know, it sounds like you're going to need some privacy when they show up here. I think I'll just wander over to The Spot and check things out from there. You need anything, that's where I'll be."

"Yeah, probably a good idea. Wish I could join you. You mind taking Morton along?"

"Not at all, it'll give me someone to talk to."

I watched out the office window as Louie and Morton crossed the street and headed into The Spot. Once they stepped inside, I settled in behind my desk, drummed my fingers on a stack of files, and waited for Tubby Gustafson to show.

Sixty-four

Louie and Morton hadn't been in The Spot for fifteen minutes when a black Cadillac Escalade pulled up and parked behind my Jeep. Fat Freddy Zimmerman oozed out of the driver's seat and waddled across the street, causing a car heading west and a city bus heading east to slam on their brakes and lean on the horn. Fat Freddy appeared oblivious. I heard him begin to pound up the stairs, but by the time he reached my door, his pace had slowed considerably, and he stepped into the office with a scarlet face. He slammed the door behind him and gasped for breath.

"You okay, Freddy? You look beat." I was seated behind my desk with my hand on the pistol that sat in my lap.

He attempted to say something, but eventually just waved me off for a moment while he sucked in more air.

"What? What the?" He gulped down more air and staggered toward my client chair with the duct tape. "What the hell did you go and tell Tubby that shit for? You, you're crazy?" he said, and collapsed in the client chair.

The chair creaked, but amazingly, held together.

"Crazy? No, I'm not crazy. But I'm focused. Two guys come in here this morning and tell me something's missing from the house you took us to yesterday and—"

"I didn't bring you, dumb shit."

"No, but you took Bono. Forced me to the curb and practically dragged him out of my car. He has to stay there for the better part of an hour while you answer questions for him, and every woman there takes a half dozen selfies with the poor guy. In case you didn't notice, I was supposed to be his damn security."

"Yeah, well, you did a hell of a job."

"Listen, these guys this morning told me to check with Tub . . . err, Mr. Gustafson. Said that whatever it was that was taken was dear to the family. I mention it to him, Mr. Gustafson, and right away, he sounds all nostalgic about a diamond necklace he gave to some guy's wife. I don't know shit about this Gatto guy, his wife, or any diamond necklace. All I know is that ever since this morning, I feel like I've been walking around with a giant bullseye on my back. Those two thugs are not going to come back tomorrow morning just to have a pleasant conversation. They mean business."

"You should have come to me. You got any idea the problem you caused?"

I could feel my fuse lighting. "Problem? You think I caused a damn problem? Well, isn't that just mighty big of you. I go out of my way to tell Tubby you were with Bono the entire time we were at that house, and now it's a problem. What the hell? I told him you had your arm around Bono and were answering all sorts of questions for him so he could save his voice for his recording session today. A recording session I might add, that he skipped in order to back up what I said about you not being involved in whatever this stupid heist was."

I sensed the wheels slowly beginning to turn in Fat Freddy's little brain.

"So, you didn't say I was involved?"

"No, of course not. Are you listening? Just the opposite. I told him you and Bono were out at the swimming pool the entire time. In fact, you want to sugar coat it, he mentioned it was some anniversary of this Gatto guy's death. Tell him you went out there to make an appearance on behalf of the organization 'cause he was tied up with the granddaughter's birthday. Everyone gets it. Well, as long as the damn necklace is returned. I'll tell you, he damn near had tears in his eyes telling me about it, that necklace."

Fat Freddy shook his head, and sort of blankly stared out the window behind me. "Damn it. I knew this was stupid right from the damn start."

"Can you get it back to them?"

"No. You're going to have to."

"Me? Why do I have to give it back to them?"

"Because, dumb shit, you're the guy they came to in the first place. They didn't ask me. They didn't ask Tubby. They told you to get back."

"That's just a minor issue. I'm nothing more than the messenger in this deal."

"Not any more. You're coming with me, now. You're gonna be the delivery boy."

"Freddy, this is a bad idea. A really bad idea."

"No, it's not. Actually, as far as I can see, it's really the only way out for me. You'll have it for them tomorrow morning. I'll be outside with a couple of guys, keeping your ass safe, letting them know if they do anything to you, it could maybe be a matter for discussion."

"A matter for discussion?"

"Stop arguing and let's go. And put that stupid gun away you're holding under the desk before you kneecap yourself. Idiot."

Sixty-five

Freddy made me climb behind the steering wheel of the Escalade. He oozed into the back seat and sat behind me. "You just drive, I'll give you directions to the country retreat, and don't do anything stupid for a change."

"The only stupid thing I did was try to cover your ass when I spoke to Tubby."

"I think you meant Mr. Gustafson. Now, just go up to the stoplight, take a right onto 35E, and head north."

From time to time, I glared at Fat Freddy in the rearview mirror or just sneered. He seemed oblivious. We'd been driving north for almost an hour and were heading into farm country when his phone rang. "Oh shit," he said when he glanced at the screen.

"Trouble?"

"You'll just keep your mouth shut and drive, if you know what's good for you," he said, waving his pistol over the headrest. After the next ring, he answered. "Yes sir. No, no, just had to pull over. I was driving and didn't want to risk an accident in the Escalade. Course some stupid son of a bitch was in my way and I—. Yes, sir. Really? Already? He did? I can do that. No, it's not a problem. I think I have a pretty good idea where he'll be right about now. I'll head over there, get him and race up there just as soon as I can. No sir not a problem. See you in a bit."

"Orders from on high?" I said, looking at Fat Freddy again in the rearview mirror. "Want me to turn around and head back to town?"

He flashed a wide grin and said, "Let's just say things have a way of working out. Tell you what, slow her down to fifty."

"Fifty? You kidding? I'm doing seventy-five and everyone is passing us like we're standing still. We'll be a damn hazard at fifty. We're liable to get rear-ended if we're not just run off the road by some nut case in a hurry."

"Well, you're driving, so make sure that doesn't happen. When we get to North Branch, take the exit and then take a right on that County road. There's a McDonald's up there, pull into the drive-up window. I could use a little snack."

"Hey, look, Freddy. I don't know if you remember, but I got a major league pain in the ass creeping up on me first thing tomorrow morning, and right now, you have me driving to Tubby's country estate. If you're not going to help me, can you at least let me pull over? You can drive yourself, and I'll hitchhike back to town. How's that sound?"

"You know, Haskell, sometimes you can be a major league pain in the ass. So 'N' 'O' spells no. Now, slow it down to fifty and take that North Branch exit, like I told you.”

It was another half hour before I took the exit. By that time, I’d lost count of how many people had given me the finger as they raced past, including a car with three kids in car seats. The mom, the dad, and all three kids gave me the finger. I took the North Branch exit, drove to the top of the hill, and turned right. There was a liquor store, two gas stations, a truck stop, and about a hundred yards further down, a McDonald’s.

“Pull into the drive-up window,” Fat Freddy said.

“I heard you the first damn time.” We waited in line, inching forward while the cars ahead of us placed their orders. Finally, we made it to the window.

“Welcome to McDonald’s, what can I get for you?” the high school girl at the window asked. She was pretty and just what you’d expect from a small-town girl in out-state Minnesota. Blonde hair, blue eyes, beautiful tanned skin, attractive figure, and a heart tattoo on her left fore-arm with the banner across the heart that read Bjorn.

Fat Freddy leaned forward from the back seat, jabbed his pistol into my rib cage, and said, “Two large strawberry shakes, two Big Macs, and two large fries.”

“I’m not hungry,” I said.

“Good, cause none of that is for you.”

“Eighteen dollars and thirty-seven cents,” the girl said.

“Go ahead, Haskell, pay the young lady.”

I looked at him in the rearview mirror, and he jabbed his pistol in my ribs again. I pulled my wallet out, and handed her all my cash, two tens.

"Keep the change," Freddy said.

"Oh, gee thanks. You're really sweet," she said and shot Freddy a big grin.

"He's a lot of things, but sweet ain't one of them."

"Pull ahead to the next window, please."

I did just that, and handed the tray with two strawberry shakes over the seat to Freddy once they were delivered. He placed them next to him and just managed to catch the bag with the Big Macs and fries when I tossed it in over the seat.

"Better watch it, Haskell. You almost knocked over my shakes. Pull into that parking space over there, put some decent music on and button your lip. I don't feel like listening to your nonstop bitching, you'll just ruin my appetite."

Sixty-six

We sat in the parking place at McDonald's with the music on while Freddy gobbled down the Big Macs and fries and drank two large strawberry shakes. I was hungry but didn't want to give him the pleasure of knowing that. He placed the empty shake cups back in the cardboard holder, crumpled the bag up, and said, "Give me the car keys."

"What? You're going to drive now?"

"Don't be stupid. Give me the keys."

I turned off the Escalade and handed the keys to him.

"Thank you," he said, using a tone that meant anything but. "Now, get this trash out of here." With that, he dumped the crumpled bag and the tray with the cups into the front seat.

I turned in the driver's seat and looked at him. "Really?"

He rammed his pistol into my ribs again and said, "Yeah, really. Come on, dumb ass, get going. We got places we gotta be."

I ran the trash to a waste bin, thought for a nanosecond about running away, but headed back to the Escalade instead. Freddy handed the keys to me once I was in and buckled up.

"Okay, I want you to take a right out of the parking lot. Stay at the speed limit. There's cops and highway patrol all over these roads."

I drove for another twenty minutes before Freddy said anything. "There's a 'T' in the road up ahead, take a left, then take the second left."

I did that. Or at least I tried to. The second left was blocked by a large red pickup truck. A guy was seated on a folding chair in the back of the pickup. No doubt a rifle at his feet. Two other guys, muscular and tan, wearing t-shirts and jeans, were leaning against the hood of the pickup. Freddy lowered his window as I stared straight ahead.

One of the guys strolled over and bent down to talk with Freddy.

"How's it going, sir?"

"Okay, under the circumstances."

"This the guy," he said, referring to me.

"Yup. He's the douche bag got everyone all wound up and out here on an otherwise nice day."

"Mmm-mmm, yeah, thanks for nothing. Right? A shame. Hey, Lenny, move the truck and let them through."

The other guy leaning against the hood hopped behind the wheel of the pickup, fired up the engine and floored it in reverse. Raising a cloud of dust and causing the guy seated in the back to grab onto the arms of the folding chair as it bounced around.

"You can pull ahead, dumb shit," Freddy said to me.

I drove down the dirt road for maybe a quarter mile, rounded a bend, and suddenly large maple trees lined either side of the road, which was now blacktopped. A white fence was behind the trees and ran the length of the green pasture on either side of the road. In the distance, two identical buildings with metal roofs sat at the end of the pastures. Three or four horses were grazing on either side of the road. A number of vehicles were parked up ahead, alongside the buildings.

"When we get past those stables up there, go to the left. Should be a black Mercedes by the house, park next to it."

I passed the stables and veered to the left. A lean-to roof was attached to the rear of the building. A couple of picnic tables were positioned beneath the roof, and a number of guys were seated or standing around in the shade. Two of them nodded in our direction, but no one waved, and none of them looked happy. A green SUV was parked off to the side, a Ford Explorer. I drove past it and pulled next to the black Mercedes.

The Mercedes was parked in front of a brick house with a large manicured lawn, a white picket fence, and a front porch. The porch had a couple of rocking chairs and two muscle-bound thugs leaning against the brick wall on either side of the front door. After I turned off the engine, Fat Freddy hopped out and said, "Let's go, Haskell."

I climbed out from behind the wheel then followed Fat Freddy through the gate and up a curvy brick path toward the front door of the house. The two thugs remained leaning against the door with their arms crossed. One of them wore a pair of mirrored sunglasses, and they both wore the same pissed-off expressions we saw around the picnic tables.

"How's it going, fellas?" Fat Freddy said and handed one of them his pistol.

"'Bout how'd you expect, not the best of days." They did a quick pat-down on Freddy then looked at me. "Why don't you move your ass over there and assume the position, dumb shit," the guy with the sunglasses said and nodded towards the brick wall between the front door and a double window.

I placed my hands above my head and leaned forward. "Spread your damn legs, asshole," he said and kicked my right foot hard, spreading my legs apart and almost knocking me over in the process.

I was about to say something, then decided to just keep my mouth closed. He patted me down, none too gently, then stepped back and said, "Okay. I guess he's in the library waiting on yous."

"Come on, Haskell," Fat Freddy said.

The other guy, still leaning with his back against the wall, casually reached over and opened the front door. As Fat Freddy walked in the house, the guy stepped away from the wall and stood so that I had to make a conscious effort to go around him. I stared at him for a long moment, then walked around him and closed the door behind us.

Sixty-seven

Fat Freddy took a deep breath and headed through the entryway and down a hall. "Follow me," he said. We passed two closed doors and stopped in front of the third door. He gave me a look that wasn't all that pleasant, took another deep breath, and knocked on the door.

"Enter," a voice I recognized as Tubby Gustafson called from inside the room.

Freddy opened the door, and I followed him in. "Good afternoon, sir," Freddy said as he closed the door behind us.

"Fast work," Tubby said, glancing at me for a half-second. He was seated behind a massive carved wooden desk that looked larger than my dining room table. "Give you any trouble?"

"No, sir, most cooperative, for a change."

"Welcome to how the other half lives, Haskell. Those of us who have our act together. Isn't that right, Freddy?" Tubby said, and raised a crystal glass filled with clinking ice cubes and a small amount of liquid.

"Correct, sir. Yes, yes," Freddy said.

"Very nice, Mr. Gustafson," I said, making a point of scanning the room and pretending I was impressed with all the shelves lined with books, the row of crystal decanters filled with expensive whiskey and the gorgeous antique desk.

Tubby drained his glass and set it on top of a file folder on his desk. "Might as well get started, he's out by the stable."

"I saw the car when we drove in," Freddy said.

Tubby shook his head and said, "Such a pity. I had hopes, plans. Just goes to show, live and learn."

We followed Tubby out of the library, back down the hall and out the front door. The two thugs had resumed their positions, leaning against the wall on either side of the door, but they jumped upright as Tubby stepped onto the front porch. "Might as well all go. You two bring up the rear," he said without stopping.

We headed down the path and over to the picnic table area where everyone was gathered. As Tubby approached, everyone rose to their feet. A number of them looked familiar to me, although if I'd ever been told their names, I couldn't remember them.

"Gentlemen, how nice of you all to join me on such short notice this afternoon. Unfortunately, I have the unpleasant task of reminding everyone what happens when we don't play by the rules. None of you are old enough to have been alive back in 1969 when my life was saved by the man who served as my mentor. A gentleman by the name of Faustino Gatto. I promised myself that I would work to find a way to pay him back, and I did."

"I was aware that Mr. Gatto adored his wife above everything else. And so, I set out to find the perfect gift to give her. Eventually, I did. The gift, unbeknownst to me at the time, afforded the financial basis for Mr. Gatto to acquire funding for his many enterprises, which, upon his death, I inherited along with his empire. I was able to do this on one provision, that his family, a wife, and son, and the generations to follow, were taken care of and at the same time removed from the business that we have all chosen. I agreed to this promise and have religiously adhered to the stipulations for the next forty years. Up until two days ago when one of our members violated those stipulations and made off with the foundation of our success, the DeBeers Lizzie Lape necklace. My gift to Giulia Gatto, Faustino's wife, a half-century ago."

"Fortunately, an individual many of you recognize as a major pain in the ass brought this incident to my attention." Tubby half-turned and raised his hand towards me. "Mr. Haskell. I have only one thing to say. No harm shall come to him over this. He did the right thing by telling me so that I could set the record straight and I've no doubt that the heavens will favor us for another fifty years for doing so."

"Let them all have a good look," Tubby said to Fat Freddy.

Fat Freddy hurried over to the green Ford Explorer, opened the rear gate, and stepped off to the side.

"All right, go ahead, take a good look. Let it serve as a reminder. This is what the hell happens when we don't play by my rules. Go on. I want everyone to see and remember."

They all sort of looked at one another then slowly walked over toward the back of the Ford Explorer, more or less forming a line in the process. Each person stopped and stared for a long moment, a number of them shook their heads. "You too, Haskell," Tubby said as one after another peered into the back of the SUV and hurried away. "Let it serve as a gentle reminder of what can happen when my rules are ignored."

I stood at the end of the line, with three guys in front of me. They each took a quick look and hurried away. I stepped in front of the rear gate, looked in, and immediately understood the message.

It was delivered by the thug with the scar across his chin. The same guy who opened the car door for Wink when we pulled up at the granddaughter's birthday party last night. He was with Fat Freddy later that evening at the Gatto mansion on Salem Church Road. Unfortunately, he looked a lot worse for the wear.

His body was laid out on a sheet of plastic. His ankles were bound with barbed wire. His shirt was splattered with blood. A look of intense pain was pasted on his face for all eternity. His hands were placed on his chest. Unfortunately, his fingers and both thumbs appeared to now be crammed into his mouth, leaving two blooded stubs. The icing on the cake was the bullet hole right between his eyes, which served as a final sort of statement. I could hear large flies buzzing around inside the vehicle.

I felt nauseous and faint and took a couple of deep breaths to steady myself. Then hurried back toward the safety of Tubby, such as it was.

"All right, everyone is free to go and get back to work. Remember, Haskell gets a free pass on this one."

The group couldn't wait to get out of there and everyone hustled to their cars. I caught the occasional glare as they hurried away. We stood and watched until they'd all driven off and sped down the road. Tubby turned toward me and said, "I have something for you. Join me for a moment back in the library." We followed him back into the house. The two thugs returned to their places, leaning on either side of the front door as Fat Freddy and I followed Tubby back down the hall and into the library.

Sixty-eight

Tubby entered his library and immediately headed over to a marble-topped cabinet with three crystal decanters, each filled with a brown liquid of slightly different shades. No doubt, very expensive whiskey. He pulled three crystal glasses off the upper shelf above the mirror and filled the first two with maybe a half-inch of whiskey. He paused and seemed to think for a moment before he returned the third glass to the shelf. He topped up one of the remaining glasses with twice the amount as the other.

He turned around, handed the glass with the smaller amount to Fat Freddy, then took a sip from the other glass, and looked at me. "So, Haskell, as you can see, there are some things I cannot abide. I don't have many rules, but the ones I have, I expect to be followed." Although he addressed me, I had the feeling the message was meant for Fat Freddy.

He set his glass back down on the marble top, pulled open a drawer, and took out a faded, powder blue case about a foot long and maybe eight inches wide. The ends of the case were carved silver. He held the case in the palm of his left hand, flipped open a silver clasp, and lifted the lid. There, resting on white silk, was the De-Beers Lizzie Lape diamond necklace.

"You'll, no doubt, guard this as if your life depends on it, because . . . well, it does," he said and laughed a maniacal sort of laugh.

Fat Freddy suddenly drained the whiskey in his glass and stood wide-eyed.

"I've contacted the Gatto family. They'll be at your office tomorrow morning, promptly at nine. See that you're there with this necklace, or the remains you saw lying in the back of that vehicle will look like a Christmas party compared to what will happen to you."

He closed the lid on the case and handed it to me. "Remember what I said, guard this as if your life depended on it because it does." This time he didn't laugh.

I took hold of the case with both hands and pressed it against my chest.

"They should be just about finished outside," Tubby said and reached into his pocket. He pulled out a set of car keys and handed them to me. "I want you to drive that car back to town, the Ford Explorer. Do with it what you will. I never thought I'd say this to you, Haskell, but thank you. Now, get the hell out of my sight."

Fat Freddy started to hurry toward the door.

"Freddy, I want you to hold on a moment. I believe we have an item or two to discuss."

"I, I was thinking I better follow Haskell back to town, provide some protection."

"That won't be necessary," Tubby said and poured maybe a quarter-inch of whiskey into Fat Freddy's empty glass. "Here, and maybe take a seat. Haskell didn't I just tell you to get the hell out of here?"

"Yes, sir, on my way," I said and headed for the door. I turned to get a quick look at Fat Freddy. The color had drained from his face. He was biting his lower lip and staring at the floor, looking like a guilty kid called to the principal's office.

"Thank you, sir," I said and hurried out, closing the door behind me. I thought for half a second about waiting to see if I could hear what was going on in the room and immediately came to the conclusion that would be a really bad idea. I tucked the necklace case inside my t-shirt and headed for the front door.

Sixty-nine

The thugs on either side of the door remained leaning against the wall. They gave me a disdainful look as I stepped outside but nothing beyond that. If they noticed the necklace case beneath my t-shirt, they didn't react.

"You finished in there," the one who'd kicked me asked.

"Yeah, he's having a little chat with Fat . . . err, Mr. Zimmerman."

"Looks like we're on," the other one said, they stepped into the house and closed the door behind them.

I hurried over to the Ford Explorer, wondering what the hell I was going to do with the body. Fortunately, although the rear gate was still open, the body was gone as well as the bloodied sheet of plastic it had been lying on. I looked beyond the car and saw a front end loader making its way across the pasture toward the tree line. What looked like an arm and a leg dangled out of the dump bucket in the front.

I quickly closed the rear gate, got in behind the wheel, fired up the engine, and got out of there just as fast as I could. I was still on the County road heading toward the Interstate that would bring me back to the city when my phone rang. Heidi.

"Hey, Heidi."

"Please, tell me you didn't forget. Remember? You were going to be here a half hour ago and move that treadmill out onto the boulevard for me."

Shit. "Forget? No, sorry, I just got caught up in some out of town business. I'm heading to your place now, but I'm still probably an hour away," I said as I accelerated, bringing my speed up another ten miles per hour.

"An hour? Okay, but don't be any later than that."

"I was going to pick up some wine."

"Oh, don't bother, I'll go get some now. You just get over here."

"Thanks, I'm looking forward to it."

"You get this treadmill out of my house, and I'll make it really worth your while." She emphasized the word really, and I increased my speed some more.

Seventy

It had taken almost two hours to drive up to Tubby's country estate, what with Fat Freddy putting me in the life-threatening position of driving fifty miles per hour on the Interstate, then cooling my heels for twenty-five minutes while he ate his little McDonald's snack. I raced back down to the city, most of the traffic was in the opposite lanes heading north, and by the time I reached the metro area, rush hour was more or less over. I pulled up in front of Heidi's in just over an hour.

I took the stairs leading up to her front door two at a time and rang the doorbell. It was turning into a pleasant evening, and her storm door was open, but the screen was locked. She stepped out of her kitchen a moment later, holding a wine glass. She was barefoot, wearing extremely tight white shorts and a grey tank top edged in white with spaghetti straps.

"Well, perfect, right on time," she said and placed a lingering kiss on my lips. "Any problems with traffic?"

"No, it was all headed north."

"Would you like a glass of wine before you move that treadmill? It's really heavy."

"Pour me a glass in the kitchen while I deal with that thing. Where is it?"

"Right where it's been for the past twenty-six months, in the den. I went ahead and removed all the clothes hanging from it. It'll be great to get that space back."

"Okay, let me get started."

"You going to need a hand?" she said sort of frowning and looking like she was afraid I might say yes.

"You know, thanks for asking, and no offense, but you might be the best help if you just went back into the kitchen and poured me a glass of wine."

That brought a smile to her face and another kiss for me. "I'll have it ready for you. Don't keep me waiting," she said and raised her eyebrows for a second and escaped to the kitchen.

I walked through her dining room and into the den. I'd set the thing up for her two years earlier. I think she used it for about a week and then started hanging items she'd ironed on it. The clothes were gone, and not surprisingly, the treadmill looked brand new.

There were four wheels on the thing, and I figured out how to get them into position in about thirty seconds. I stood behind the treadmill and pushed it out of the room toward the front door using my foot. I had to move the dining room table and the chairs off to the side of the room, but that was about it. In the process of moving the table, I realized I still had the case with the necklace tucked inside my t-shirt. I set the case on the dining room table then rolled the treadmill out to the front door.

I bought her a doorstop for her screen door a couple of years ago. A cast iron dog raising its leg, so when it was against the door, it looked like the dog was peeing on the door. She hated it at first, but after all the funny comments from friends, now she tells everyone she picked it out. I opened the screen door, put the doorstop in place, and half lifted and rolled the treadmill out the door.

The thing felt like it weighed about a thousand pounds. I lowered it down the four front steps, one at a time. Fortunately, it didn't damage or scrape the stone. I pushed it onto the front lawn then rolled it out and onto the boulevard. All in all, it didn't take me more than ten minutes.

"Need a hand?" she said when I walked into the kitchen.

"No, already out there."

"What?"

"Hey, you've got the master doing the work for you. Did you tell me you were going to print off a sign?"

"Got it right here," she said and handed me a sheet of paper.

FREE for loving family!
No return.

Two pieces of tape were attached to the top of the sheet.

"Let me just stick this on the front of that thing, and I'll be right back." I hurried out and taped the sign to the front of the treadmill. I hadn't even made it back to the house when a car came down the street with two twenty-somethings, they slowed to almost a stop and studied the treadmill. I figured it would be gone before we were finished with dinner.

I went back inside. Heidi was in the dining room, returning the chairs to their original position. The jewelry case was still sitting on the table.

"Lift the end of that table, and we can put it back just the way you like," I said.

We moved the table maybe two feet placing the legs back exactly over the indentions on the oriental rug.

"How 'bout that wine?" I said.

She looked at me, then the jewelry case, and looked at me again.

"Okay, you get me that wine, and I'll show you what I've been dealing with," I said.

She picked up the case, and we headed into the kitchen.

Seventy-one

Heidi drained the last of her wine and pushed the empty glass across the kitchen counter so I could refill it. "So this gangster gave the necklace to the guy's wife and the guy, the wife's husband, wasn't upset? The wife didn't run off with the gangster?"

"Well, I think by that time, she was probably old enough to be his mother or even his grandmother."

"Well, okay, but still, I mean, so what? What is this thing worth?" She placed her hand over the necklace. She'd been wearing the thing for most of the past hour after only wanting to 'try it on for just a minute.'

"What's it worth? Okay, first of all, the one you're wearing is based on some original work of art type of necklace by this DeBeers place. Still, I didn't get the thing estimated and don't have the time, but it's supposed to be worth somewhere between one and a half and three and a half million. At least that's what it said about the original necklace online."

"And he just gave it to this guy's wife?" she said and gently rubbed her hand across the diamonds for the umpteenth time.

"Apparently, as a gift, yeah. Just remember, we're not dealing with what you and I would consider normal people here. These are crooks. I'm not going to investigate, but it would be interesting to learn how he got it. Somewhere in the background, there's gotta be a robbery, a murder, something, probably a number of shocking things that wouldn't be a surprise."

"But still," she said and rubbed her hand over the diamonds again. She had placed a small makeup mirror on the counter, right after she turned off the dinner and said we could eat later. The mirror was on a chrome stand with a built-in light, and had a normal view from one side, and if you spun the mirror over, a magnified view on the other side. She'd already taken a half dozen selfies, not counting the four photos she'd had me take.

My stomach growled, it had been doing that for the past hour, but Heidi was focused on her reflection in the mirror again. "I'm just trying to think where, exactly, you could wear this. You'd have to have a half dozen armed guards with you, and even that might not be enough."

"Maybe, you could wear it to dinner. Hey, what an idea. How 'bout we have dinner, since I'm starving, and you can wear the necklace."

"Oh, God. Food, sex, and beer, is that all you ever think about?"

"No, I like this wine and Jameson whiskey, too."

"All right, I suppose I better take it out of the oven."

"You sure, it's only been in there for about four hours."

"Do you want to eat and then stay for the erotic dessert course, or would it be better if Mr. Crabby just went home?"

"I'm staying, I'm staying. I was just thinking that if we ate, not only could you tell people you wore the necklace, but you could tell them you wore it to dinner."

She seemed to think about that for a long moment, then quickly opened the oven door and brought out a pan of I didn't quite know what.

"Hmm-mmm, boneless pork ribs, do you think they're supposed to look like this?" The ribs were shriveled and looked bone dry beneath the dried out, blackened BBQ sauce.

"They look fine," I lied, so hungry I didn't care. "Tell you what, think of it as a fancy restaurant dinner, and we're going to eat it no matter what, and you're the best looking woman in the place, and you're wearing that necklace. Everyone is turning to look at you as the maître d' pulls out the chair for you."

"But I'm in these shorts and a tank top, Dev."

"Yeah, and they're all staring at your fantastic figure and the really cool guy you're with."

"I thought you would be with me?"

"Very funny. More wine?"

Seventy-two

I woke up in Heidi's bed. The digital clock read 3:45, and her side of the bed was empty. I heard a noise from the far side of the room, rolled over, and caught just a sliver of light seeping out from beneath the bathroom door. I waited.

Now the digital read 4:05, and she was still in the bathroom. Every once in awhile, I would hear her bump into something, close a drawer, or open a cabinet door. I finally couldn't stand it, got up, and knocked on the bathroom door.

"Heidi, you okay? Everything all right?"

"Yeah, yeah, fine. Hang on. I'll be out in just a minute."

After five minutes, I sat down on the bench at the end of the bed next to two outfits I didn't recall being there when we'd gone to bed and waited. Eventually, the door opened, and she stepped out of the bathroom. She was wearing a black cocktail dress, low cut, with a large velvet bow at the base of her cleavage. I remembered it from the night we went to an anniversary party at some swanky place down on the St. Croix river last Christmas. She had her arms wrapped around a bundle of at least a half-dozen different outfits. She dragged them over to the bench and dumped the pile on top of the two outfits already there.

I glanced at the clock, "Honey, it's after four in the morning, what in the hell are you doing?"

"This is the only night of my life I'm going to be able to wear something like this. I just wanted some pictures to remember it by, that's all."

"You've been in there photographing yourself wearing the necklace with different outfits?"

"Yeah, well, at least some of the photos, others might have been of a more personal nature."

"That part sounds great, but how long have you been in there?"

"Well, since you conked out about sixty seconds after you were finished, I don't know, I guess a little before midnight. Of course, I had to do my hair and makeup. As long as I'm taking pictures, I figured it might be nice if I looked my best."

"Heidi, you always look your best."

"Oh, aren't you sweet," she said, not meaning a word. "And apparently, last night wasn't enough, just what are you all of a sudden thinking about this early in the morning?"

"I just wish I could let you keep it. I really do."

"Oh, that's sweet of you, but know what? One night, wearing it while we made love, and I got to dress up, that's enough for me. It was fun, but with the criminal history, maybe there's a bad vibe from this thing. I'm going to go back to bed. What time did you say you had to have this back?"

"Those two guys are supposed to be at my office at nine."

"Okay, it's mine until seven-thirty, then you get it back, fair?"

"Yeah, I guess that works. Without a doubt, you're the most gorgeous woman to ever wear that."

"Aw, thanks," she said. "Come on, let's go back to bed. I got an idea I think you're gonna like."

Seventy-three

Heidi's alarm clock went off a little after seven. She rolled onto her side, pulled the pillow over her head, then, while half-asleep ran her hand over the necklace just to make sure it was still there. I crawled out of bed, grabbed a shower, dressed, then gently shook her. "Breakfast in thirty minutes, Heidi. Time to get up."

I had the dinner dishes washed, the coffee on, and bagels in the toaster when she came into the kitchen. She gave me a kiss, turned around and said, "Unhook me and send me back to my boring life."

"You are anything but boring," I said, as I unhooked the necklace and placed it in the case on the kitchen counter.

"Fun for a night, but that was all I needed."

She was quiet during breakfast, but then again, I was only there for another twenty minutes, and she was going on just a couple hours of sleep. I wanted to get down to the office early before the Gatto guys arrived. We kissed in the kitchen, and I watched her wander back to her bedroom. I let myself out, stood on the front porch, and stared. Now there were two treadmills on the boulevard.

No point in telling her, she'd find out soon enough, so I headed down to my office.

As I pulled in behind my Jeep, I noticed a black Cadillac Escalade a few spaces up. My first thought was the Gatto's were twenty minutes early, but then the driver's door to the Escalade opened, and a pair of legs gingerly swung into the street. Fat Freddy gradually pulled himself out of the driver's seat and cautiously headed toward me. He was clearly moving with a good deal of pain. He had a white plastic brace wrapped around his neck and a wide velcro belt around his mid-section. His eyes were black, his nose looked freshly broken, and his swollen lips seemed to have a blue tinge to them. He had a plastic boot on his right leg that extended from his foot to up above his knee.

"Haskell, wait up a minute," Freddy groaned.

I watched as he slowly limped a couple more steps in my direction before I moved toward him.

"Freddy, what the hell happened? You okay?"

"Ahh, I'll live, I think. Little bit of a misunderstanding, sort of guilt by association."

"What?"

"Mr. Gustafson thought I might have been a party to the incident with the necklace."

I remembered being out by the swimming pool when the guy with the scar across his chin gave Freddy the nod that it was time to leave. My guess was Tubby was right, Freddy had probably been involved. Somehow, he must have done some pretty fast talking.

"But you worked it out, everything okay?"

"Well, it will be in time, I hope. I got this boot for about six weeks, and I'm not too sure on the neck brace. I promised Mr. Gustafson I'd be down here to provide security for you until the Gatto's showed up to grab that necklace. Where is it by the way?"

"In a safe place, not to worry."

"You going to meet them in your office? I'm not sure I can handle the stairs, you got going up to that flea pit."

"Might be best if you just stayed in your car. That way, you can keep an eye on whatever direction they come from. They were driving a black Escalade the other day, just like the one you got."

"Well, that'll make them easy to spot," he said and began to laugh. His laugh quickly turned into a wince of pain. "Yeah, sort of sounds like staying out here on the street might be the best idea. I'll maybe stay in the car and check things out. Guess you better head up there. Don't worry. I got your back out here on the street."

"Appreciate that, Freddy. You rest up."

"You maybe might mention to Mr. Gustafson that I kept an eye on things this morning, you know, put in a good word for me."

"Yeah, not to worry, I'll be sure to do that," I said, then watched as Freddy slowly made his way back to his car. He opened the driver's door, then sort of eased up against the seat, leaned back and groaned as he hoisted himself up, and in, behind the wheel before he closed the door. So much for security.

I went back to the Ford Explorer, picked the blue bag off the floor labeled DOGGY DOO that held the necklace case, and hurried across the street. Twenty minutes later, a black Cadillac Escalade parked right in front of the building door, across the street from my Jeep and the Explorer. I recognized the two guys the moment they climbed out of the car. They quickly glanced up and down the street. If they noticed Freddy parked a half-dozen spaces up the street, they gave no indication before they headed into the building. A moment later, I heard them coming up the stairs. They knocked on the door as they entered.

"Gentlemen, welcome," I said and flashed a broad smile. They looked around the room, the shorter of the two stepped over to the file cabinet and checked the far side, not that anyone could squeeze into a two-inch space.

"You spoke with Mr. Gustafson." The taller one said, making a statement rather than asking a question.

"Yeah, I did, more than once. I gotta tell you, I didn't get the necklace returned."

They gave me a suspicious look. "But we were told, that—"

I held my hand up, cutting him off. "Relax, you'll get it. I just want it understood that I'm only the messenger here. I don't know how or why it was stolen. I can tell you this. It didn't work out well for the individuals involved. Mr. Gustafson was very clear that this was not a good idea, and there would be hell to pay should anyone think of trying to take it again. Can I ask you something?"

"Maybe?"

"From what I understand. Part of the arrangement between Mr. Gustafson and Faustino Gatto was that the family would never be involved in the business that Faustino was involved in and that Mr. Gustafson operates today."

"That's correct."

"So, if you don't mind me asking, who are you guys?"

They looked at one another, and then the taller of the two said, "Faustino Gatto was our grandfather."

"But you're in the business?"

"The business? You mean criminal activity? Oh, hell no. I'm a gastroenterologist," the taller one said.

"And I run a software firm," the other said. "Mr. Gustafson has always served as a family advisor."

"Tubby Gustafson, is your family advisor?"

"Tubby?" they said in unison.

I watched them out the window as they climbed back in their car and drove off with the necklace. A minute later, Fat Freddy started his car and drove away.

Epilogue

There was a knock on the door just before lunch. "Yeah, come on in, door's open." It took me a moment before I recognized him. His head was shaved, he was wearing a Minnesota Wild t-shirt and shorts, and he'd ditched the earrings and glasses. "Wink?"

He held out his arms like he'd just been announced on stage. "Hey, Dev. So, what do you think?"

"I didn't recognize you, man. When did you do all that?"

"You kidding, about thirty minutes after you dropped me off. I got to thinking on the way home. That Tubby guy with the chicks feeding him, the guy is nuts man, and he tells me I better leave town and get my ass out to Hollywood and make a record. Spare me. Anyway, I figured it was fun while it lasted, but too much screwy stuff went along with it. The woman who pierced my ears. That massage gal in the shower room. I don't even want to mention Sassy. Don't get me wrong. I enjoyed it for a while, but then, all those bad guys and the way things were going. It was starting to be more bad stuff than fun stuff."

"So, you're done being Bono?"

"Yeah. Hey, dude, it's a lot less stressful. Mind if I interrupt your boring day and buy you lunch? If you got time."

"You got a deal. Come on. The Spot does pizza right across the street."

Just as I got up from my desk, my phone signaled a text message coming through. I clicked on the screen, Heidi. I opened her message. A selfie, Heidi wearing just a smile and the necklace with the word "THANKS."

Wink caught a quick glimpse and said, "Wow, who is that hottie?"

"She's private. Come on, let's grab that pizza."

The End

Thank you for taking the time to read **Star Struck**. If you enjoyed the read, please consider taking a moment to leave a review. Even if it's just a few words it really, really helps. Thanks…

Don't miss the following sample of **International Incident**, the next work of genius in the Dev Haskell Private Investigator series.

Sneak Peek

International Incident

Second Edition

MIKE FARICY

One

I was looking forward to dinner at Heidi's. It seemed for the past couple of weeks we could never get together. Either she was busy or said she needed a night just to herself. I'd been working on an insurance fraud case and had finally put it to bed.

A guy claimed he'd been injured in a car accident. The problem was it was his third such injury in as many years. He claimed to have been rear-ended, but in all three cases, the accused drivers testified that he had backed into them as they drove down the ramp onto the interstate.

Tommy Brennan was a high school pal who now worked as an investigator for an insurance company. He caught the case about three months back, sent it my way, and it rang a bell. A little research on my part came up with a similar lawsuit from the same individual two years earlier. After backing into the other vehicle, always a senior driver, the 'victim,' Delbert Downder, would sue for twenty grand. His lawsuits carried the stipulation that if it wasn't settled quickly the cost of medical procedures, treatments and rehab could easily exceed a hundred grand. What insurance company wouldn't settle for one-fifth of that?

Anyway, with some sterling investigation on my part, Delbert Downder was charged and decided to threaten me. The end result was I'd received a nice check from the insurance company, and Downder was serving time. As a celebration, I arrived unexpectedly at Heidi's front door with two bottles of her favorite wine, rib-eye steaks, and hopes of a memorable evening.

"Hey, you're early I . . . Dev?" Was all she said when she answered the door. She wore a shocked look on her face. She stood frozen in the process of inserting a diamond earring in her left ear. Suddenly, I had the distinct feeling it hadn't been me she was expecting to see. She wore tight white slacks and a red silk top. She stared at me with wide eyes and her mouth hanging open.

"Hi, Heidi. I got your favorite wine, and your favorite steaks, and I was hoping to cook you dinner. It looks like you might have other plans. You can keep working, watch TV, or sit and talk to me. I was thinking it would be great to spend an evening with you and—"

"Umm, this is a really bad time. I've got a meeting tonight, and it's going to run very late."

"Oh, yeah. Well, I tried to call you, but I kept on getting a recording that said you were unavailable. I couldn't even leave you a message. I just figured you might be busy, and I was hoping maybe I could help. Mind if I come in and just put this stuff in the fridge? We could get together tomorrow night or maybe the night after that. You know, whatever fits your schedule. No pressure."

She gave a quick look up and down the street and said, "Come on in for a minute. We need to talk."

We need to talk. Whenever a woman has used that phrase on me, things have never gone my way. Okay, sometimes I probably deserved it. Maybe most of the time. But not now, not tonight. I followed her into the kitchen.

Despite the fact that Heidi was possibly the worst cook in the world, the kitchen was filled with a wonderful aroma. There was a large pot on the stove and two white Styrofoam trays in the wastebasket. Two takeout meals she'd no doubt claim as her own work. The dining room table was set for two, and the candles were lit. Adele was on her sound system singing about being alone with someone.

"Oh, ahh, it looks like your meeting is here. Sorry to interrupt. I didn't know you—"

"Oh, Dev. I'm so, so sorry. I was going to tell you. I just didn't know . . ."

"It's okay, Heidi. I get it. Hey, look, you might as well keep these steaks and the wine. You know, put it to good use. Maybe your guy can fix dinner tomorrow night."

"I'm sorry, Dev. I was going to tell you. It just all happened so fast I didn't know how. Umm, can you wait just a minute? I've got something for you."

"You don't have to give me anything, Heidi. I'm just sorry. I shouldn't have come over without—"

"Here," she said, opening the pantry closet. She handed me a cardboard box for twelve bottles of wine. Only it held two plastic paint trays, my paint roller, and a couple of brushes. As I took the box, she reached back into the pantry and grabbed a brown paper grocery bag by the handles, and handed it to me. Boxers, a couple of t-shirts, some socks, my St. Paul Saints sweatshirt and a pair of my running shoes.

"Oh yeah, thanks. This is great. I've been looking for this stuff."

"Oh, Dev."

"No, really. Don't worry about it, Heidi. We're both adults. I wish you all the best. I better get out of here before your guest arrives." I made a beeline for the front door. Carrying the wine box and the grocery bag, I turned and pushed the screen door handle using my hip. I looked at Heidi, gave her a wink and a smile, and made tracks to my car before she saw the tears.

I tossed the cardboard box and the grocery bag into the back seat of my car, a '91 Ford Escort. The driver's door was taped closed so it wouldn't fall off. I had to open the front passenger door and slide over the console into the driver's seat. The car started on the third try, and I headed down the street. Just as I got to the corner, a red Lexus LC came around the corner and headed up the street. It was an expensive, sporty looking thing with a large chrome grill. I watched in the rearview mirror as it came to a stop right in front of Heidi's house. A moment later, some guy wearing a dark suit and open-collared shirt climbed out. He reached back into the car and grabbed a bouquet of white flowers. Probably roses. He waved toward the house, which suggested Heidi was still standing at the door, watching. It looked like she'd done pretty well for herself.

TWO

Three weeks later.

"No. You're not listening, sweetheart. Now, I want you to stay right here in bed. I'm going to make you breakfast, and then I'm going to bring it into you. We'll have breakfast in bed, and, well, who knows what might happen after that. Now sit up for a second."

Maddie had just finished law school. Her hair was dyed yellow, not blonde, but a bright yellow that faded into green for the last inch or two. It was all kinky curls and hung down to her shoulders. She wrinkled her nose and gave me a kiss. As I sat up, she pulled her pillow on top of mine and sort of fluffed them up before gently pushing me back. She gave me a quick peck on the cheek and rolled out of bed. She searched around on the floor before she found her thong and pulled it on.

The thong was red with a cut out in the shape of a heart in the front. She stepped over to the nightstand on her side of the bed, picked up the TV remote, and tossed it over to me. "Here Dev, you can watch the news. I'll be back with breakfast in five minutes. Don't go any-where," she giggled and wrinkled her nose again.

I wanted to pull her back into bed. "You sure I can't give you a hand?"

"No, it will be a lot better if you stay right there. This will only take a couple of minutes."

"Don't take any longer than that. I'm missing you already."

She giggled, grabbed her cellphone, and began texting as she strutted out of the room.

I didn't feel like watching the news. It was more like twenty-five minutes before she returned. She was carrying a large wooden tray with two plates and two mugs of coffee. Both plates featured a stack of three pancakes drowning in an ocean of syrup and three sausages. Her eyes were focused on the tray, walking slowly, taking tiny steps as she came around to my side of the bed.

"Here can you take this?" She said, placing the tray on my lap. The coffee mugs were literally filled to the brim, and as she set the tray down, a wave of steaming coffee rolled over the side of both mugs and onto the tray. She seemed not to notice, hurried around the bed, and climbed in on her side.

We'd had three dates over the past two weeks. Last night, following another party, we came back to her apartment for, *'A little glass of wine.'* We never had the wine. In fact, I'm not even sure she had any wine in her apartment. Not a complaint, by the way.

Along with the yellow-green hair she had deep brown eyes and a lacy little tattoo on her tail bone that read 'Welcome'. I didn't bother to comment.

"Okay, dig in," she said.

I carefully handed a plate over to her, followed by a knife and fork. She sat next to me with her legs crossed, and the plate balanced on her lap. "Say, would you mind turning that cartoon off? It's kind of distracting, and it's starting to give me a headache."

I clicked off the TV and tossed the remote on the bed. "You sure the headache isn't from the margaritas you were drinking last night."

"Mmm-mmm, that too, probably," she said and stuffed some pancakes into her mouth.

I cut a wedge from my stack of pancakes, took a bite, and almost got sick. The things tasted burnt.

Maddie reached for her coffee mug, and as she took a sip, I lifted the top pancake on my stack. The one in the middle was blackened, and the bottom one looked charred.

"How's the breakfast?"

"Umm, good, Maddie. Very good. What's not to like about breakfast in bed?" I stabbed one of the sausages with my fork and cut off a bite. It was cold. Not cold like it had been out of the pan too long, but cold, as in nearly frozen. It sort of crunched as I bit into it.

Maddie placed her plate on the nightstand next to the bed, apparently finished after two bites. She held her coffee mug in one hand, her cell phone in the other, and wore a big smile. I was focused on her little red thong. "Good?" She asked, not bothering to look up. She was sending a text to someone using just one thumb to quickly crank out the message.

"Delicious," I replied. I took the tray and carefully set it on top of the chest of drawers on my side of the bed. I took hold of the coffee mug, settled back on the two pillows, and took a sip as I faced her. It was instant coffee, lukewarm instant coffee.

"That's all you're eating?" She said, scrolling through messages.

"I can eat, or I can sit here and study how beautiful you are."

She smiled, set her mug on the nightstand next to her plate, and curled up next to me. "Everyone was right. You are full of shit. But that was sort of sweet. You know, I'm going on that trip to Paris right after my graduation ceremony. I just wanted to let you know I'm really going to miss you." She went back to texting, this time using both thumbs.

"Well, if it makes you feel any better, I'm going to miss you, too. But you'll love Paris. Have you ever been?"

"To Paris? No, I've only been out of the country twice, both times fishing in Canada with my dad and brothers. I've been to California and Florida, but this will be my first time to Paris. I can't wait. You sure you can't come?"

I took that as a compliment. We chatted for another minute or two. Maddie suddenly raised her eyebrows and climbed on top of me. Just as it seemed to be getting very interesting, her cellphone signaled a text coming through. She continued to move rhythmically, reached for her phone, and proceeded to send a reply. Apparently, she was a master at double-tasking. After a replay of our late night activity, she told me she had to get ready for a meeting. I got dressed and headed out the door. On my way past the kitchen, I happened to notice the package of frozen pancakes next to the toaster and the sausage package next to the microwave.

Three

I left Maddie's a little before nine. It turned out her luncheon meeting was with an uncle. She actually referred to him as her favorite uncle. She was going to do some sort of pro bono work for him since he had apparently paid her law school tuition. I wasn't sure she really grasped just how wonderful he was to do that for her. I made a mental note to try and meet him in the near future.

As I pulled in front of my house, I saw Morton standing on the couch, looking out the window. He began barking as I slid across the console and stepped out of the passenger side of the car. Morton met me at the front door. No sooner had I stepped inside the house than he literally ran to the back door, barking all the way. Morton's translation probably would have been something along the lines of, "It's about time." I barely opened the back door before he shot across the porch and into the yard. He spun around in a circle a couple of times and assumed the position, all the while giving me a disgusted look.

After the midnight and morning workout with Maddie, not to mention no breakfast, I was starving. I scrambled a half dozen eggs, made some toast, and put on a pot of real coffee. Morton and I had breakfast together, I showered, and we headed down to the office.

My officemate, Louie Laufen, was sitting at his desk, actually a picnic table, when we arrived. The table was covered with a number of files. Louie was leaning back in his chair with his feet up on the table. He was on his phone, and he gave me a nod as we entered. Morton headed toward his bed in front of the file cabinet, and I opened the second drawer on my desk, pulled out my binoculars, and scanned the apartment building across the street. Louie finished his phone conversation just as I finished scanning the apartment windows across the street.

"Hey, Dev. Any luck?"

"No, it's already after ten. Everyone's already gone off to work."

"Actually, I meant your date last night."

"Oh, yeah, had a really great evening. Yet another party of folks she said she went to law school with. Not that anyone wanted to talk about it. I didn't know any of them, and once they found out what I do for a living, they weren't interested in knowing anything more about me."

"Yeah, it'll be party time for all of them for about a week. But believe me that damn bar exam is already hanging over their heads. Some of them will try and take the exam in July, but if they're anything like my class, the vast majority will be shooting for February. Sounds like a long way off, but in short order, the damn thing is here. You know when this Patty is looking to take it?"

"Patty dumped me a couple of months ago. This girl is Maddie, Louie, and no, she hasn't mentioned the bar exam. She had to hurry and get ready for a meeting this morning. She's going to be doing some pro bono stuff for her uncle. Get this. The guy paid her law school tuition."

"Her uncle paid her tuition? That's a good chunk of change and an awfully nice thing to do. Does he have some big company or somewhere she's going to be working at?"

"I don't know. She never really mentioned him before. She didn't actually say much except that he paid her tuition. Anyway, that's why we had to cut things short this morning. She has a luncheon meeting with him today. In fact, she's probably heading there right about now."

"What'd you say his name was?"

"I didn't. She never told me, and with the exception of this morning when she kicked me out of her bed, I can't recall another time she's ever mentioned him. Probably some guy into high tech internet stuff, or a doctor, or something."

"Or maybe he's a judge or practices himself. You ever find out who he is, let me know. At the end of the day, it's still a pretty small community, and I can maybe give you an update on the guy."

"We'll see what develops. We've only gone out a couple of times."

"Which is probably why she's still interested in you. Wait until she gets to know you a little better, she'll run screaming for the nearest exit."

Four

Louie left the office for a court appearance around two that afternoon, another DUI case. Driving Under the Influence. If you were arrested for driving under the influence in this town, Louie Laufen was the guy you wanted to represent you. He'd become Mister DUI in the city, not that he'd ever been arrested for it. Well, actually, he had been once, but he got off on a technicality, so it never appeared on his record.

I had a cop pal who told me once that most people, after a couple of drinks, think, 'I better wait for a while and not have another drink before I head home.' But if you've had seven or eight drinks, you're probably going to order one more for the road and figure you're okay to drive.

Louie said the guy he was representing had been arrested twice before in the past three years. The best scenario was going to be jail time, a revoked license, and a substantial fine. That was before they increased his car insurance if he could even get insurance. Jail for one to three years and car insurance for about a grand a month for the next ten years after that was a hell of a price to pay for being stupid about drinking.

After Louie left, I took Morton for a quick walk around the block. I deposited the dog poop bag in the trash can in front of my building and headed back up to the office. Morton sat in front of my desk, waiting for the dog biscuit he always got after our afternoon walk. Once I tossed him the biscuit, he lost all interest in me and headed over to his bed alongside the file cabinet. I grabbed the binoculars and did an early scan of the apartment building across the street. Nothing shaking.

I was about to replace the binoculars in my desk when a car pulled up and parked across the street right behind my Ford Escort. It was a large SUV, a black Cadillac Escalade to be specific. It wasn't the chrome spinning wheel hubcaps, or the windows tinted darker than the law allowed that caught my attention. Unpleasant experiences began to flood my memory. When the driver's door opened, a massive male figure oozed out of the seat and looked up at me, staring out the window. All my hopes were dashed, and it was already too late to hide.

Fat Freddy Zimmerman saw me and flashed me the finger as he walked around to the passenger side of the Escalade. Along the way, he spit on the trunk of my car. He opened the rear passenger door for his boss, local crime lord Tubby Gustafson. Tubby appeared to groan as he slid out of the back seat, and the large car rocked from side to side. He stepped onto the sidewalk and took a moment to adjust his tie.

Fat Freddy appeared to whisper something to him. Tubby glanced up at me, staring down at the two of them. He gave me the finger as he proceeded to cross the street and headed for the door to my building. Great minds think alike.

A car sped down the street and had to slam on the brakes to avoid hitting Fat Freddy and Tubby. Thankfully, the driver didn't honk. Instead, he just nodded politely when Freddy gave him a look. They disappeared from sight, and a moment later, I heard the staircase begin to creak. I listened to the two of them groan and wheeze as they headed up the stairs. I hoped somehow Freddy and Tubby might be headed for an appointment at the hairdressers just across the hall from me. No such luck. All was quiet for a few seconds until a red-faced Fat Freddy held the door open. The city's crime lord, Tubby Gustafson, stepped in.

He had a look on his face, more disgusted than usual, as he glanced around the office. He shook his head, waddled up to my desk and waited for Freddy to pull the client chair out.

Morton looked up and apparently recognized all six hundred plus pounds Tubby and Fat Freddy brought to the table. He simply lowered his head and placed his paws over his eyes. Who could blame him? Tubby glared at me with cold blue eyes. His nose, the size of a baked potato, was red and pocked marked. It looked as if someone with football spikes had stomped on it a couple of times.

"Apparently, some things never seem to change," Tubby said, as he settled into the client chair. The chair creaked, suggesting it might break into kindling at any moment. He indicated the binoculars I was still holding with a wiggle of his chins. I quickly placed the binoculars into an open desk drawer and pushed it closed with my knee. "I see you've done absolutely nothing along the lines of sprucing up this dump. Sit down, Haskell. You're making me nervous standing there, pretending to think. Does it hurt?"

I didn't answer his question. "To what do I owe the pleasure of a visit, Tub . . . er, umm, Mister Gustafson?"

"Oh, please. Spare me the attempt at manners. I have a bone to pick with you."

"Me? What have I . . . Mister Gustafson I haven't seen you for the better part of a month, possibly two. I've been investigating people for the past three weeks for an insurance company. Just making sure their resumes and employment applications are correct. I've been involved in nothing on the criminal end of things. Not that I consider you a criminal, sir. I haven't talked to the police or federal authorities, and I certainly haven't mentioned your name to anyone else." Why bother, I thought.

"Collateral damage, Haskell."

"Excuse me?"

"Get your head out of your ass and listen up."

"Oh, I heard you, sir. It just isn't making any sense."

"No doubt because you make such a damn mess of everything you touch. After a while, I'm sure it all just runs together for an idiot of your ilk."

"Maybe if you gave me a clue, sir."

"A clue? How about the name Madeline Swanson."

Jesus Christ, Maddie? My late night erotic cuddle? Breakfast in bed Maddie? Maddie in the red thong with the perfectly placed heart cutout? Maddie with the welcome sign tattooed just above her gorgeous rear end? Maddie with the yellow and green hair? "Madeline Swanson, sir?"

"Don't play stupid with me, Haskell. You're so damn stupid you can't even play stupid well. Yes, Madeline Swanson. My niece, by the way."

Oh no. Not good. "Well, I know a Madeline Swanson, a law school student. I mean, she was a student. She just finished law school. As a matter of fact, she's graduating with honors. This weekend."

"She is graduating Summa Cum Laude. Do you even know what that means, Haskell?"

"Umm, that she's really brilliant?"

"It means that she's too good for the likes of you and your contemporaries. Now, after all her hard work and my investment, the poor thing has unwittingly presented me with a problem."

"A problem, sir?"

"Yes, you dunderhead. A very big problem. Namely you."

"Oh, sorry sir. I didn't know. I mean, maybe if I explained to her that we're acquainted perhaps that would, umm, help to eliminate the problem."

"Acquainted? You're missing the point, as always. I don't want the likes of you to have anything at all to do with my niece."

"You mean, we should stop seeing one another?"

"Good Lord. If only it was that easy. No, Haskell, that's too damn abrupt. You're going to let her down easy. Do you understand?"

"Down easy. Yes, sir."

"Now, she's graduating at the weekend after which she's off to Paris for some sightseeing."

"I knew about her trip. I mean, she told me she was going. That will be the perfect time for her to get me out of her mind and I can pretend to be busy when she gets back to town and—"

"Silencio, you moron. You'll do no such thing. I'm sending you to Paris on the same flight. You'll act as her bodyguard for the week. This will be perfect. You can report to me every day. Give me an update on her activities. God forbid she'd actually meet someone nice over there," he said and looked me up and down.

"Paris, Mister Gustafson?"

"Yes. Have you ever been?"

"No, sir."

"I don't suppose you speak French?"

"No, sir."

"Even better. You'll just follow her around and not get in the way. I'll be booking you a separate room in her hotel. Other than carrying her luggage, you're not to

touch her or anything belonging to her. Do I make myself clear?"

"Yes, sir. But, Paris? I mean, are you sure? I've got
work lined up and I—"

"Haskell, please do not present me with one more
problem. Work lined up? Maybe instead of a week in
Paris, you'd prefer a two week stay in a hospital, in trac-
tion. Do I make myself clear?" He paused for a moment
before shouting, "Well, do I?"

"Yes, sir. Very clear."

"One other thing. You are forbidden to attend her
graduation ceremony or the reception that follows. She's
worked damn hard, and I'm not about to have the likes
of you ruin the event. Should you decide to show, you
won't live to see the sunset. Questions?

"No sir, understood."

"God, the things I do. Come along, Freddy. Get me
out of here before I follow my instincts and eliminate
Haskell as a problem once and for all. And Haskell, God
help you if you even think of mentioning this conversion
to Madeline. I find out you so much as mentioned this to
her, and we can skip the hospital stay and focus on a pau-
pers grave. Capiche?"

Fat Freddy pulled the chair back as Tubby stood. He
walked to the door, turned, and looked like he was about
to say something. After a long moment, he simply shook
his head and growled, "Oh, what in the hell is the point?"

Fat Freddy followed him out the door and down the
stairs. I watched from the window, waiting for the two

of them to exit the building and appear on the street below. Tubby stepped off the curb in front of the bus that
was pulling over to pick up two passengers. The driver
slammed on the brakes but didn't honk the horn. Fat
Freddy hurried across the street and held the rear passenger door open for Tubby. He closed the door once Tubby
settled in. He looked up at me staring out the window
and gave me the finger again before he climbed in behind
the wheel. The tinted windows were so dark that once
the doors were closed I couldn't see either one of them.
A moment later, the Escalade was racing up the hill. I
stood and watched out the window until it disappeared
from sight.

To be continued...

Oh great, Tubby Gustafson and Fat Freddy Zimmerman can probably bypass TSA at the airport. With that
as a sendoff who knows what's going to happen when
Dev travels. No doubt some sort of **International Incident.** Better grab your copy, **NOW!**

Books by Mike Faricy

Crime Fiction Firsts

A boxset of the first four books in four crime fiction series:

Russian Roulette; Dev Haskell series
Welcome; Jack Dillon Dublin Tales series
Corridor Man; Corridor Man series
Reduced Ransom! Hot Shot series

The following titles comprise the Dev Haskell series:

Russian Roulette: Case 1
Mr. Swirlee: Case 2
Bite Me: Case 3
Bombshell: Case 4
Tutti Frutti: Case 5
Last Shot: Case 6
Ting-A-Ling: Case 7
Crickett: Case 8
Bulldog: Case 9
Double Trouble: Case 10
Yellow Ribbon: Case 11
Dog Gone: Case 12
Scam Man: Case 13
Foiled: Case 14
What Happens in Vegas… Case 15
Art Hound: Case 16
The Office: Case 17

Star Struck: Case 18
International Incident: Case 19
Guest From Hell: Case 20
Art Attack: Case 21
Mystery Man: Case 22
Bow-Wow Rescue: Case 23
Cold Case: Case 24
Cash Up Front: Case 25
Dream House: Case 26
Alley Katz: Case 27
The Big Gamble: Case 28
Bad to the Bone: Case 29
Silencio!: Case 30
Surprise, Surprise: Case 31
Hit & Run: Case 32
Suspect Santa: Case 33
P.I. Apprentice: Case 34
Rebel Without a Clue: Case 35

The following titles are Dev Haskell novellas:
Dollhouse
The Dance
Pixie
Fore!
Twinkle Toes
(*a Dev Haskell short story*)

The following are Dev Haskell Boxsets:
Dev Haskell Boxset 1-3
Dev Haskell Boxset 4-6
Dev Haskell Boxset 7-9
Dev Haskell Boxset 10-12
Dev Haskell Boxset 13-15
Dev Haskell Boxset 16-18
Dev Haskell Boxset 19-21
Dev Haskell Boxset 22-24
Dev Haskell Boxset 25-27
Dev Haskell Boxset 28-30
Dev Haskell Boxset 1-7
Dev Haskell Boxset 8-14
Dev Haskell Boxset 15-19
Dev Haskell Boxset 20-24
Dev Haskell Boxset 25-29

The following titles comprise the Jack Dillon Dublin Tales series:
Welcome
Jack Dillon Dublin Tale 1
Sweet Dreams
Jack Dillon Dublin Tale 2
Mirror Mirror
Jack Dillon Dublin Tale 3
Silver Bullet
Jack Dillon Dublin Tale 4
Fair City Blues
Jack Dillon Dublin Tale 5

Spade Work
Jack Dillon Dublin Tale 6
Madeline Missing
Jack Dillon Dublin Tale 7
Mistaken Identity
Jack Dillon Dublin Tale 8
Picture Perfect
Jack Dillon Dublin Tale 9
Dublin Moon
Jack Dillon Dublin Tale 10
Mystery Woman
Jack Dillon Dublin Tale 11
Second Chance
Jack Dillon Dublin Tale 12
Payback Brother
Jack Dillon Dublin Tale 13
The Heist
Jack Dillon Dublin Tale 14
Jewels To Kill For
Jack Dillon Dublin Tale 15
Retirement Scheme
Jack Dillon Dublin Tale 16
The Collector
Jack Dillon Dublin Tale 17

Jack Dillon Dublin Tales Boxsets:
Jack Dillon Dublin Tales 1-3
Jack Dillon Dublin Tales 4-6
Jack Dillon Dublin Tales 1-5

Jack Dillon Dublin Tales 1-7
Jack Dillon Dublin Tales 6-10

The following titles comprise the Hotshot series;
Reduced Ransom! Second Edition
Finders Keepers! Second Edition
Bankers Hours Second Edition
Chow Down Second Edition
Moonlight Dance Academy Second Edition
Irish Dukes (Fight Card Series)
written under the pseudonym Jack Tunney

The following titles comprise the Corridor Man series:
Corridor Man
Corridor Man 2: Opportunity knocks
Corridor Man 3: The Dungeon
Corridor Man 4: Dead End
Corridor Man 5: Finger
Corridor Man 6: Exit Strategy
Corridor Man 7: Trunk Music
Corridor Man 8: Birthday Boy
Corridor Man 9: Boss Man
Corridor Man 10: Bye Bye Bobby

Corridor Man novellas:
Corridor Man: Valentine
Corridor Man: Auditor
Corridor Man: Howling

Corridor Man: Spa Day

The following are Corridor Man Boxsets:
Corridor Man Boxset 1-3
Corridor Man Boxset 1-5
Corridor Man Boxset 6-9

All books are available on Amazon.com
Thank you!

Contact the author:
- Email: mikefaricyauthor@gmail.com
- Twitter: @Mikefaricybooks
- Facebook: Mike Faricy Author
- Website: http://www.mikefaricybooks.com

Published by

MJF Publishing

www.ingramcontent.com/pod-product-compliance
Lightning Source LLC
Chambersburg PA
CBHW071407200726

48294CB00002B/307